Sharon Gasped As Though He'd Just Removed Her Most Intimate Garment—

"I like to see a person's eyes when we're talking," he told her dryly. He held her sunglasses up. "Why do you feel you have to hide behind these?"

"I'm not hiding from anything," she returned defensively. She moved to get her glasses back, but he held them out of her reach.

He smiled wryly. "Then why do I get the feeling you're hiding a deep, dark secret?"

"Because you have an overactive imagination," she shot back.

He twirled her glasses slowly, thoughtfully. "No, I don't think so." Probing amber eyes searched hers. "There's something behind your eyes. They look...haunted."

He leaned across the table toward her, "I told you *my* deep, dark secret last night," he said, his voice low and deep, disturbingly intimate. "Why won't you tell me yours?"

Dear Reader,

Welcome to Silhouette! Our goal is to give you hours of unbeatable reading pleasure, and we hope you'll enjoy each month's six new Silhouette Desires. These sensual, provocative love stories are both believable and compelling—sometimes they're poignant, sometimes humorous, but always enjoyable.

Indulge yourself. Experience all the passion and excitement of falling in love along with our heroine as she meets the irresistible man of her dreams and together they overcome all obstacles in the path to a happy ending.

If this is your first Desire, I hope it'll be the first of many. If you're already a Silhouette Desire reader, thanks for your support! Look for some of your favorite authors in the coming months: Stephanie James, Diana Palmer, Dixie Browning, Ann Major and Doreen Owens Malek, to name just a few.

Happy reading!

Isabel Swift
Senior Editor

SDRL-7/85

GINA CAIMI
Branded

Silhouette Desire
Published by Silhouette Books New York
America's Publisher of Contemporary Romance

SILHOUETTE BOOKS
300 East 42nd St., New York, N.Y. 10017

Copyright © 1986 by Gina Caimi

All rights reserved, including the right to reproduce
this book or portions thereof in any form whatsoever.
For information address Silhouette Books,
300 East 42nd St., New York, N.Y. 10017

ISBN: 0-373-05308-8

First Silhouette Books printing October 1986

All the characters in this book are fictitious. Any
resemblance to actual persons, living or dead, is
purely coincidental.

SILHOUETTE, SILHOUETTE DESIRE and colophon
are registered trademarks of the publisher.

America's Publisher of Contemporary Romance

Printed in the U.S.A.

GINA CAIMI

started making up her own fairy tales when she was six years old. It was the only way she could get through arithmetic class. She sculpts as a hobby, adores the opera, ballet and old movies, but writing remains her major passion. And she still hates arithmetic.

One

She certainly didn't look like a cold-blooded murderer, Ross was forced to admit when he'd zoomed in on a tight close-up of her face. There were no drapes on her bedroom window, and the spotless glass was invisible in the darkness, affording him a clear view from the cabin across the way. Her pale face appeared luminous in the amber glow from the lamp on her night table; she looked like a child—a frightened child.

For a moment he wondered whether the woman he held trapped in his viewfinder was the right one. Sucking in a fast, hard breath, he quickly snapped several shots of her. The harsh clicks, the soft whirring of the camera, the only sounds in the pitch-black room.

Sharon sank back against the brass headboard and closed her eyes, waiting for her heart to stop pounding, for the constriction in her chest to ease up so she could breathe normally again.

What was she so afraid of? Ross wondered, zooming in so close he could see the tiny drops of sweat making her skin glisten. She'd gotten off scot-free. Or was it guilt? Why else would she be hiding in a quiet little town like St. Michaels, almost three thousand miles away from the scene of the crime? And why had she gone to such lengths to change her appearance and identity if she wasn't guilty of murder?

Leftover shreds of the nightmare seeped through to Sharon's consciousness like a bloodstain through a white shirt, enveloping her until she felt as if she were suffocating, as if all four walls of the room were closing in on her. She tore the covers off and jumped out of bed. Pausing only to slip into her mules, she rushed out of the bedroom.

Following the trail of lights she left in her wake, Ross moved from window to window, holding in front of the one directly across the way from her living room. Camera poised, he waited for her to settle down.

With a shaky hand, Sharon turned on the TV. A burst of machine-gun fire shattered the silence and her already frayed nerves, making her jump. She didn't have to look at the picture to know that it was a cop show rerun. She'd been in Maryland less than three weeks but she already knew every show that aired after 1:00 a.m. by heart.

She quickly switched to the late movie in the hope of seeing a forties comedy or musical. She didn't recognize the film that was playing; from the costumes, heavy shadows and heavier organ music, she assumed it was a Gothic melodrama. At that point she was willing to watch just about anything as long as it distracted her from the memory of the nightmare that still clung to the edges of her mind. She wondered why the nightmares had started again and when they would stop. Maybe moving into her late husband's former home hadn't been such a good idea after all.

Ross continued to watch her intently through the zoom lens. He waited until she'd settled into the overstuffed armchair in front of the television set before he shot several more close-ups of her. Suddenly, as if the overhead light wasn't bright enough to dispel all the shadows in the room, she reached up and switched on the large reading lamp flanking the armchair. The reading lamp was ten times brighter than the bed lamp had been, exposing her as mercilessly as the glare of a spotlight during a police grilling.

She certainly was a tiny little thing, not even five foot three. From the press photos he'd expected her to be taller and not quite so frail. She looked like a kid trying on her mother's clothes in that huge, loose-fitting white cotton nightgown she was wearing. He would have thought that someone like her went in for the slinky black lace variety. She wasn't at all what he'd expected, he realized irritably. Once again he wondered whether he had the right woman.

Balancing the camera in one hand, Ross reached over and lifted the newspaper clipping out of the file folder he'd left open on the desk earlier in the evening. With the tip of the zoom lens he carefully pushed the drapes apart a few more inches, letting the reflection of the full moon spill through the slice of window onto the clipping.

WIFE SHOOTS BUCK STARR DEAD IN "FREAK ACCIDENT," accused the banner headline. The image of the woman looking up at him from the front page—all false eyelashes and exotic makeup, long, thick, dyed black hair teased to glamorous heights—was as different from the woman he'd just been studying as two people could be.

Will the real Sherri Starr please stand up? Ross thought wryly as he peered through the viewfinder again. He couldn't help feeling that she looked more attractive this way, definitely more appealing.

The long, black hair was now a soft, warm brown and cut as short as a boy's. The scraggly-cut ends spilled onto her forehead, down the sides of her face and neck, emphasizing what the French would have called a gamine quality. She looked younger at twenty-eight than she had at twenty-five. Her features were too offbeat for her to be a beauty, yet they came together in a way that was far more intriguing than perfectly even features could ever be. The false eyelashes and exotic eye makeup were gone as well, and her slanting brown eyes seemed even larger in her pale face. But there was no way she could change that crazy-looking mouth.

"Thank God for that," Ross found himself muttering under his breath. She had just about the sexiest mouth he'd ever seen. The slightest overbite made her full lips look as if they were always puckered up, just waiting to be kissed. It was an invitation he knew most men would find difficult to resist, one that was impossible not to fantasize about.

With a harsh sigh, Ross tossed the clipping back on the desk. He could see now why even a rock star idol who could have practically any woman he wanted had fallen so hard for her—hard enough to marry her—hard enough not to realize that she was capable of destroying him.

The full, high curve of her unconfined breasts filled the viewfinder as she moved abruptly to get to her feet. The resulting white blur was caused as much by his hand jumping as by her bounding out of the armchair.

Choking back sobs, Sharon rushed over to the TV set and shut it off, blanking out the horror movie she'd been watching. Coming on top of her nightmare, the ghastly scene she'd just witnessed was more than she could handle. How could people view violent death as entertainment? she wondered angrily. Maybe if they knew what it was really like to stand by helplessly and watch someone you love bleed to death . . .

Sharon wrapped both arms around her middle, trying to hold back the familiar feeling of panic that was churning up the acid in her stomach and starting to burn a corrosive path up her throat as images from the nightmare she was no longer able to suppress flooded her mind.

There was blood everywhere. She never knew that a body could hold so much blood. Buck was writhing on the carpet and she didn't know what to do. Suddenly, a towel appeared in her hands. Kneeling down, she pressed it against the wound trying to staunch the flow of blood but the white towel was soaked through in seconds, dyed a warm sticky red. The wound kept getting wider and wider and the towel began sliding out of her hands as if it were being sucked into a whirlpool. Frantically, she fought to hold on to it but the suction was too strong for her. As if in slow motion, the towel slipped through her fingers. She watched it disappear into the gaping hole. Blood began gushing out again. In desperation, she pressed her hands against the frayed edges of the widening gash to hold it together. Suddenly, she felt her hands being sucked down, deeper and deeper, into the raw, gaping wound. . . .

Sharon cried out, as she always did at that point, trying to break free of the nightmare—except that she was wide-awake now. Her arms tightened around her stomach. Was she going to start having nightmares when she was awake, too? She'd thought she'd finally put all that behind her.

What the hell was going on with her? Ross wondered as he continued to study her in amazement. She was shaking

uncontrollably and her eyes were glazed with terror. It was
a reaction he was used to seeing from victims, not murderers. He cursed himself for a fool. Like most criminals trying
to hide a guilty past, she obviously lived in terror of being
found out. It was his job, he had to remind himself, to see
that she *was* found out.

Determined not to give into the emotions threatening to
overwhelm her, Sharon took several long, deep breaths but
that only made her dizzy. There wasn't enough air in the
room. Once again, she had the sensation that everything was
closing in on her. Impulsively, she hurried over to the front
door and pulled it open. A gust of wind rushed in to greet
her. Only then did she remember that she was in her nightgown. Yanking her trench coat off the bentwood coatrack
that stood next to the door, she quickly slipped it on, wrapping it around her without bothering to button it. Twisting
the belt impatiently into a single knot, she stepped outside.

She didn't realize that she was drenched in sweat until she
felt the tiny dots of water turn to ice on her skin as another
unseasonably cold gust of wind swirled around her. But it
was so much easier to breathe outside. Drawing the fresh,
pine-scented air deep into her lungs, Sharon started across
the grassy slope that led to the water's edge.

"What's she up to now?" Ross muttered between
clenched teeth. Going over to the door, he opened it just
enough to get the wide lens through. She was heading
straight for the cabin. It occurred to him that she must have
spotted him somehow in spite of all his precautions. Just as
he was trying to figure out what to do next, she turned and
walked down to the pier, which was at the foot of the embankment directly in front of the cabin.

A fresh gust of wind coming off the water knifed through
Sharon's trench coat and whipped her nightgown around

her legs, making her shiver. A native of Southern California, she still wasn't used to the colder temperatures of the eastern seaboard, and it had been an unusually cold and rainy June. The chill, which she hadn't realized had sunk deep into her bones from sitting, damp with perspiration, in the cold living room wearing only a cotton nightgown, was now spreading to the rest of her body.

In spite of the cold, Sharon welcomed the wind's assault on her senses; it forced her to deal with reality and cleared her mind, blowing away the last fragments of her dream. As the wooden slats creaked under her feet, she continued resolutely to the end of the pier.

Ross saw the almost desperate determination in her step, and it made him uneasy. What in hell was she doing out on a pier in her nightgown in the middle of the night in the state that she was in?—unless . . .

His breath caught and he shifted his position in the doorway in order to get a clearer look at her just as the moon was swallowed up by a cloud, plunging everything into darkness. When his eyes became accustomed to the dark, he was able to make out a tiny, huddled form leaning over the wooden railing at the end of the pier.

Fascinated by the strange, almost fluorescent light skimming the surface of the dark water, Sharon strained over the railing to get a better look. As the full moon slipped through the shadowy web of clouds trying to hold it captive, her attention was caught by the silvery shimmer of a chain. One end was wrapped securely around one of the end posts, the other disappeared into the dark waters. Curious, she bent down to see what the chain was attached to—it seemed to be some kind of cage—but she was still too far up to get a good look at it.

A curse escaped Ross when he saw her step through the opening in the wooden railing. Balancing herself precariously on her toes, she hung poised over the very edge of the pier. One hand reaching up to grip the railing, she was staring into the black depths of the water as if it held a fascination she was unable to resist. Suddenly, Ross knew exactly what she was doing out there, what she was just desperate enough to try. Without thinking, he slung the camera strap over one of the pegs on the clothes tree next to the door and went rushing outside.

"Hey, hold it!" he yelled as he went tearing down the grassy embankment. "What do you think you're doing?"

With a startled cry, Sharon turned her head and saw the tall, shadowy figure of a man rushing toward her from the other end of the pier. Her ankle twisted under her, causing one slipper to fall off, and she lost her balance. Her nails grated on the wooden slats like chalk on a blackboard as she lost her grip and plunged into the water.

The instant shock to her nervous system as the frigid waters closed over her made it impossible for Sharon to recover quickly enough. Time stopped, became an eternity, as she found herself sinking deeper and deeper into the blackness surrounding her. Then, just as her lungs felt as if they would burst from lack of air, her survival instinct took over, moving numb limbs and propelling her back up to the surface. She was vaguely aware of a loud splash as a dark form knifed into the water.

She'd always been an excellent swimmer but she was unable to fight the powerful current, which had already dragged her several hundred feet away from the pier. Her trench coat was heavy, threatening to drag her under again. Treading water, she managed to untie the belt with boneless fingers. The coat was quickly swept away by the current.

Still gasping for air, Sharon was trying to judge how far away she was from the shore when she saw the man swimming rapidly toward her. She'd never been so glad to see anyone in her life. She made an effort to swim toward him but her arms and legs were numb from the cold; all she succeeded in doing was to thrash around in one spot. With a few long, sure strokes, he was by her side.

"I've got you," he muttered as his arm went around her waist, pulling her effortlessly up against him. "Get onto my back and—"

"No, I . . . I should be able to—"

"Get on my back," he ordered harshly, "before we both freeze to death." It was the wrong moment for her to assert her independence but at least, Ross realized with grudging admiration, there was no danger of her panicking. "Put your arms around my neck and hold on tight."

Without another word, she obeyed him. Time seemed suspended. A sense of unreality overcame Sharon as she clung to the lean, hard body beneath her. Eyes closed, she floated on top of him, lulled by the sure, rhythmic movements of his body while he swam back to shore.

"What kind of crazy stunt was that?" he demanded the instant they touched solid ground.

"Stunt?" Sharon shot back defensively. Any gratitude she might have felt because he'd rescued her vanished as she remembered that it was his fault that she'd fallen into the water in the first place. "If you hadn't come . . . screaming out of the darkness," she stammered, "like a . . . a banshee . . ." Confusion clouded her mind, making it difficult for her to put the words together. " . . . I never would have . . ." Vaguely, she realized that she was slurring her words. She stumbled and if his hand hadn't been there to catch her, she probably would have fallen.

Ross recognized the early symptoms of hypothermia instantly. "Come on, we've got to get you warm and out of those wet clothes." He tugged on her arm and she staggered clumsily again.

"Wait, I...lost my slippers," Sharon murmured thickly, staring down at her bare feet. She giggled when she found that she couldn't lift her feet if she wanted to. Why were they so heavy? The wind came up, shaking the pine trees that studded the embankment, ripping through the wet nightgown that was plastered to her body. In a kind of daze, she wondered why she didn't feel cold anymore.

"Come on!" Quickly, Ross bent down and swept her up in his arms. "There's no time to lose."

"Hey, whas the—?" Sharon started to protest but the sure, hard support of his arms, the way he was holding her felt oddly reassuring. She let her body sink against his. Her arms were as heavy as lead when they went up to circle his neck. Pulled down by sheer weight, her head fell onto his shoulder.

Ross stiffened when he felt the softness of her breasts against his chest. Their clothes were soaking wet, glued to their bodies like a second skin—they might as well have been naked. Didn't she realize that he could feel every part of her? What was she trying to pull now? He slanted her a quick, wary look. In the bright moonlight, her face was soft and trusting, and she was snuggling up to him with an unself-conscious innocence as if she were merely seeking his warmth and protection. To his amazement, he found that he wanted to protect her.

With a silent curse, he reminded himself who she was. He was sure that, somewhere in that steel trap of a mind of hers, she knew exactly how seductive she looked and felt, and just how appealing most men would find her "helplessness." He should have let her drown, he told himself angrily as he carried her swiftly up the embankment toward the house. She certainly had it coming to her after what she'd done.

Cradled securely in his arms, Sharon found herself sinking into a delicious drowsiness that suffused her senses. Her eyes fluttered closed and her breathing grew deep and heavy.

"Don't go to sleep!" he ordered sharply, his rough voice exploding in her ear, shattering her languorous daze.

Sharon's head snapped back and she looked up at the man who was yelling at her so rudely while holding her with a tenderness she'd never known. When she finally got her eyes to focus, she studied him curiously. There was a lean, hungry look about him. The look of a predator. The icy moonlight emphasized his stark features, the hard set of his jaw. His narrowed eyes were as yellow as a cat's—a jungle cat's. If it hadn't been for his surprisingly sensitive mouth and the way he was holding her, she might have been afraid of him.

"Good thing you left the door open," he muttered gruffly. With his foot, he kicked the door open the rest of the way and carried her over the threshold. "My God, it's almost as cold in here as it is outside." Impatiently, he kicked the door shut behind them.

With long, quick strides, Ross crossed the living room, heading for the bathroom. He knew where every room in the house was down to the last closet. He realized that he should have pretended otherwise so as not to blow his cover but there was no time to lose. He could see that she was fighting to stay awake, and her breathing was becoming slow and shallow.

A sigh of regret escaped her when he set her back on her feet, propping her up against the tile wall next to the sink. Rushing over to the old-fashioned bathtub Ross ran warm water in it as fast as the old brass fixtures would allow.

"Jus' what do you think...you're doin'?" Sharon demanded, clinging to the edge of the sink with numb hands because she could barely stand.

Ross smiled crookedly. She certainly had plenty of grit. His face hardened when he reminded himself that committing cold-blooded murder required plenty of grit. "You know what hypothermia is?" he asked bluntly.

She stared at him blankly before shaking her head.

"Well, that's what you've got, take my word for it." Bending over the edge of the tub, he tested the water to make sure it was the right temperature. "And if we don't get you warm, fast, you could slip into a coma...then, death." He smiled sardonically over his shoulder. "You do know what death is, don't you?"

Her eyes widened. Yes, she knew what death was. She nodded slowly.

"Then you'd better get out of that wet nightgown." Ross caught his breath when he turned and got a full-length view of her in the bright light. Her high, round breasts were clearly visible through the soaking wet, white cotton fabric that the water had rendered transparent. Nipples, taut from the cold, gleamed wetly, making his pulse jump. Though he tried not to, his eyes moved down her body, lingering over the swell of her hips and the softly rounded curve of her belly.

The burning intensity of his gaze broke through Sharon's dazed state. She gasped when she followed his glance and saw the reason for his reaction. Her fingers still numb, she tugged at the nightgown, trying to detach it from her body.

Ross laughed. Who was she kidding? A woman like her didn't know the meaning of the word modesty. "Come on, get out of that thing before you freeze to death," he ordered, his voice hard. But when he turned his back on her again, and reached over to turn off the faucets just as the tub was about to overflow, his hands were unsteady.

"You can go now," Sharon assured him, her words slurring as if she were drunk. "I can...handle this." The effort it took to undo the top button of her nightgown with fingers that refused to work caused her to stumble. She slipped in the puddle of water at her feet but he was there to catch her.

"This is no time for false modesty," he grated, pushing her hands out of the way. Not bothering to undo the tiny pearl buttons running down the front of her nightgown, he ripped them open and tore the gown off her with one impatient motion.

Sharon cried out but was too stunned to do anything else. She'd never felt so vulnerable and exposed in her life. Before she could recover, he'd swept her up effortlessly into his arms and was carrying her over to the bathtub.

With more willpower than he knew he possessed, Ross kept his eyes glued on the water. He'd gotten enough of a glimpse of her body through the wet nightgown to know just how lovely and exciting she must look naked. He didn't need her to take his mind off his job any more than she already had. But he was unable to stop the jolt of desire that shot through him when he felt her trembling in his arms.

Quickly, he lowered her into the tub of warm water.

Two

Sharon sank down into the bathtub as far as she could go. She wished she could sink right through the enameled bottom of the tub and disappear into a hole in the ground.

"That's right, try to get in the water as deep as you can," Ross told her, pulling a towel off the rack. When he noticed the frantic way she was trying to cover herself with her arms, he realized that she was more concerned about hiding her body, which was clearly visible through the transparent water, than she was about getting warm.

With a perplexed frown, he stepped behind the head of the tub. Using the towel, he began rubbing her scalp to dry her soaking wet hair and get the blood circulating.

Sharon tensed automatically. She was about to protest, but the sure, strong feel of his hands, the delicious warmth that was radiating from them felt too good to complain about. Her neck muscles went slack again.

Ross felt her relax under his hands. A long, ragged sigh escaped her and her eyelids fluttered closed, but she kept her arms wrapped tightly around her body. A bemused smile tugged at the corners of his mouth: a modest murderess?

"Why did you do it?" he asked flatly.

She tensed again, and her eyes flew open. He was sure that he saw a flash of fear in their dark depths. "Do... what?"

"Try to take the long swim to China."

"Is that what you thought, that I wanted to kill myself?" She laughed breathlessly, even a little brokenly, and the tension disappeared. "No, you startled me and I...I lost my balance."

"But what were you doing out on the pier at this time of night in the first place?" Swinging the towel over his shoulder, Ross slid his fingers into the short, damp strands of her hair. Slowly, he began massaging her scalp.

"I couldn't sleep," Sharon murmured, the warmth of the water, the slow rhythmic movements of his fingers drawing the chill out of her, making her drowsy. Her eyes closed.

"Keep right on talking." The tone of his voice, which she just realized held the slightest trace of a Southern accent, was as hypnotizing as the warm, supple fingers that were now working their magic on the nape of her neck. "Why couldn't you sleep?"

"Because I'd had a terrible—" A warning bell suddenly went off in Sharon's head. She'd been grilled too many times not to realize when she was being pumped for information. She pulled her head away, breaking his hold on her. The abrupt movement sent water spilling over the edge of the tub.

Turning her head, she looked up at him. Their eyes met for the first time, and held. The breath caught in her throat.

She'd seen eyes that unique shade of amber in a human only once before. For a moment, she wondered whether she was hallucinating. Silently, he continued to hold her gaze.

Sharon swallowed convulsively. "Who are you?"

Ross saw the fear drain what little blood was left in her face. There was a wild look in her eyes, like that of an animal caught in a trap. Suddenly, he felt ashamed. "Don't be afraid. You have nothing to fear from me," he assured her, meaning it, somehow, even though he knew that it wasn't true. "Are you feeling any better?"

"Yes," Sharon breathed, looking away. The concern that was now softening his eyes was almost as disturbing as the hardness she'd thought she glimpsed in them before. She'd been through so much in the past three years, she was becoming paranoid. The man had saved her life, after all, and there was no way he could know who she was or that she would be out on that pier tonight....

But she'd trusted helpful "strangers" before, she reminded herself, only to be betrayed every time. "Yes, I'm feeling much better now, so you can—"

"I'll be the judge of that," he cut her off sharply. Coming around the curved end of the bathtub, he studied her face intently for a moment before placing his hand flat on her cheek.

Sharon flinched when she felt the heat from his palm on her skin. How could he be so warm when he was still dripping wet and the bathroom was so damp and chilly?

"You're still cold," he said, feeling her other cheek, "but not as bad as before." Trailing warmth, his fingers slid down to the base of her throat where they felt for the pulse. He frowned. "Give me your wrist."

Sharon's arms tightened defensively about her naked body. "What?"

"Give me your wrist." He held out his hand impatiently. "I want to feel your pulse."

"Are you a doctor?" Sharon demanded, hoping rather foolishly that he was. His manner was as irritatingly superior and impersonal as any doctor's.

He laughed wryly. "Do I look like a doctor?"

She stared up at him, seeing him clearly for the first time. The work shirt and battered jeans he wore were sopping wet and clung to a tall, sleekly muscled body. There was something of the loner about him. She couldn't see him sitting behind a desk in an office. With his stark face and hard, rangy body, he could have been a cowboy—or a bounty hunter.

There was a fierce intelligence behind his eyes; probing eyes that weighed everything as carefully and precisely as he weighed each word before he spoke. Somehow, she knew that his judgements of people were sure, swift and irreversible. Deep lines edged his mouth and the corners of his eyes but they weren't the result of aging; he couldn't have been more than thirty-five. She had the feeling that he'd seen more of life—the raw, tragic side of life—than he would have liked, and it had left its mark on him.

"No, you don't look like a doctor."

"Well, I'm not." When she still hesitated, he plunged his hand into the water, and grabbing her wrist, pulled her arm away from her breasts and out of the bathtub with one impatient motion.

"What do you think you're doing?" Sharon cried angrily, struggling to cover her entire body with only one arm and not doing a very good job of it. "Let go of me!"

"You *are* feeling better," Ross drawled. His fingers gripped her wrist securely as he checked her pulse beat against his wristwatch. Out of the corner of his eye, he caught tantalizing glimpses of her body through the rippling water. He didn't need anyone to take *his* pulse to know it was speeding up.

"I may not be a doctor," he informed her, trying to keep his voice even, his manner strictly impersonal, "but I've had a lot of emergency first aid training so I know how to take a pulse." He dropped her arm back in the water. "Yours still isn't normal. You'd better stay in there another ten minutes or so." Sliding the towel that he'd used to dry her hair off his shoulder, he began rubbing his own sopping wet hair.

Though she found his cool, impersonal manner reassuring, Sharon tightened her arms around her body.

After combing his fingers through his damp locks, he began rolling up the towel. "Meanwhile, I'll get a fire going to warm up that living room, and I'll hunt down some dry clothes for you."

"I can do that my—"

"You stay right there," he cut her off. Moving back to the bathtub, he bent over and lifted her head.

"Now what are you doing?" she asked, her tone defensive and feaful at the same time.

She certainly wasn't the trusting type, Ross noted. He wondered why. "I just thought the edge of the tub might be a bit hard on your neck," he returned wryly as he slipped the rolled-up towel under her head.

She turned her face toward him, bringing it within inches of his. With large, wary eyes she looked at him as if she wasn't used to thoughtful gestures unless they were prompted by ulterior motives. She smiled suddenly, a soft, tentative smile that was all the more sensuous for not trying to be so. "Thanks."

Ross straightened up like a shot. "It's okay," he muttered. "Now you stay in there, you hear?" Turning quickly, he made for the door; he let out a sigh of self-disgust when he'd shut it behind him.

Sharon let her head sink back against the improvised terry cloth pillow. Now that she was alone, she was able to let her body relax completely. Her arms floated down to her sides She hadn't realized how exhausted she was. Closing her eyes, she gave herself up to the warm water that was melting the heaviness in her limbs, slowly bringing feeling back to them.

An unusual scent began to pervade her senses—the light smell of wildflowers and another, darker smell like musk. She recognized the lighter one as her cologne; the muskier scent must have rubbed off him when he'd used the towel to dry his hair.

The image of his lean face flashed in her mind, lingered behind her eyelids. Sharon reexperienced the warmth of his hand on her skin, the feel of his strong arms cradling her body. She tried to concentrate on the healing warmth of the water, but the mingling scents continued to swirl around her.

After getting a good strong fire going in the living room, Ross headed for the kitchen to make them both something hot to drink. Searching through the cabinets for a jar of decaffeinated coffee, he found several boxes of herbal tea.

Nature's Cure For Insomnia proclaimed the flowery inscription on top of the boxes, The Natural Way To A Good Night's Sleep.

So she was having trouble sleeping, Ross noted with satisfaction when he saw that there were less than half a dozen tea bags left in the open box. He remembered how surprised he'd been to see the light go on in her bedroom after 1:00 a.m. He was sure now that it was guilt that was preventing her from sleeping. That was what she'd been trying to run away from when she went rushing out of the house in her nightgown.

A sardonic smile twisted his mouth. She obviously had something remotely resembling a conscience, after all. As he filled the copper teakettle with tap water and placed it on the burner, he made a mental note of that: her sense of guilt could make it easier for him to trap her.

While he waited for the water to boil, Ross searched through the contents of her refrigerator. You could tell a lot about a person from the type of food they bought. What he found was exactly what he'd expected from a woman like her: cold cuts, frozen hamburgers, an assortment of cheeses. He was sure that she hadn't cooked a decent meal in her life.

Sharon shifted languorously in the bathtub, stretching her legs until her toes touched the enamel edge. The warm water had melted the chill in her bones, all the numbness in her limbs; pins and needles pricked her fingers and toes, making them tingle. The veil of confusion that had clouded her mind was lifting as well, bringing the events of the last half hour into shockingly clear focus. There was a strange man in her house! A man who had stripped her naked and was now out doing God only knew what!

Grabbing the curved edge of the bathtub with both hands, Sharon pulled herself up out of the water. A shiver went through her as she felt the chilly air on her heated flesh. She swayed when she stepped down onto the bath mat and had to grip the edge of the tub again to steady herself. Her body ached to sink back into the healing warmth of the water but her will was stronger. She wasn't going to be lying naked and passive in the bathtub when that man came back.

Sliding the large bath towel out of the antique brass ring attached to the tile wall, Sharon dried herself with quick, angry motions.

She couldn't believe this was happening to her; she was beginning to think she was jinxed. With a sigh of frustration, Sharon wrapped the towel securely around her as she started for the door. She'd thought she'd finally put trouble behind her, three thousand miles behind her. Now, more trouble—in the lean, hard shape of a man with piercing gold eyes and surprisingly sensitive hands—was waiting for her just beyond that closed door. Her fingers froze as they were about to turn the doorknob.

Ross managed a quick scan of the newly decorated living room as he carried two steaming mugs of herbal tea over to the fireplace. She certainly hadn't wasted any time making herself at home he thought bitterly, remembering how the old place used to look. A more thorough study of the room would have to wait until later. *He* didn't have any time to waste either.

Taking a couple of quick gulps of tea to ward off the chill beginning to sink into his bones from his wet clothes, Ross set both mugs down in front of the crackling, blazing fire. Getting warm would also have to wait until later. He knew from experience that most people tended to keep their most secret and intimate possessions hidden away in the bedroom.

A sudden thrill of anticipation shot through him, surprising him as he crossed the living room in a few impatient strides. It made him wonder whether his eagerness to find out as much as he could about her was merely professional curiosity. Pausing in the doorway, he glanced down the hall. The bathroom door was still closed.

Like a sliver of wood embedded deep under his skin, the awareness of her lying naked in the bathtub irritated him. All the more so because he couldn't get at the source of his irritation. What was it about her that made it so difficult for him to keep a cool head?

He couldn't remember when a woman had called to his senses so quickly or so intensely. There was something about her eyes, that incredible mouth. The feel of her delicate body cradled in his arms, the soft crush of her breasts as she snuggled up against him still tugged at his senses, propelling him into her bedroom with a raw curse.

Her heart beating erratically, Sharon eased the bathroom door open and peered outside. The hall was deserted. Holding her breath, she listened intently for any sound that might tell her where he was and what he was doing. There were no sounds; the house was as silent as a graveyard. Still, she hesitated.

It wasn't like her to be such a coward. If the man had meant to take advantage of her, she told herself with perfect logic, he would have done so when she was lying helpless and naked.

She clutched the bath towel tightly around her. It wasn't fear that held her frozen in the doorway, Sharon suddenly realized, but the fact that she now had to face the man who had stripped her. A shiver went through her as she recalled—no, not recalled—reexperienced the way his eyes had moved over her body, hunger and heat burning right through the wet fabric that had clung, transparent, to every inch of her.

In the dazed state she'd been in she might have just imagined his reaction, Sharon tried to reassure herself. Though used to admiring glances from men, she'd certainly never seen one of such raw, sexual intensity. It was as if an electric shock had gone through her, strong enough to penetrate the daze that . . .

No, she hadn't imagined it. Nor had she imagined her own reaction to it—then or now.

She was tempted to step back into the bathroom and lock the door behind her but she refused to let a stranger force her to hide in her own house. Besides, he was a man in his prime, it was only natural for him to react to the sight of a practically naked woman. Later his manner toward her had been cool and impersonal, downright impeccable.

Somehow, Sharon didn't find her rationalization as reassuring as she would have liked. But she knew that she had to face the man sooner or later—she had to get him out of her house! Clutching the towel around her with both hands, she stepped out into the hallway. The oak floor felt as cold as a slab of marble under her bare feet as she tiptoed toward her bedroom.

Slowly, silently, Ross slid open the top drawer of the dresser. Quickly, his hands skimmed through the neatly folded stacks of lingerie, searching for anything that might be incriminating—letters, drugs, a gun. All they found were lacy bras and panties and the satin shimmer of slips.

His fingers tensed when they suddenly located something stuffed into one corner of the drawer. It felt like a pouch of some kind, probably a stash of drugs. Pulling it out, he lifted it to his nose and took a good, hard whiff of it. Expecting the pungent smell of marijuana, Ross was thrown by the delicate scent of dried flowers—wildflowers. An unexpected surge of heat went through him: it was the same fragrance he'd caught a whiff of when her head had fallen onto his shoulder.

With a muffled curse, Ross stuffed the sachet back into the corner of the drawer. He was about to shut the drawer when curiosity got the better of him. What kind of lingerie did she wear? The more he knew about her, the easier it would be to break down her defenses and get the proof he needed to convict her, he told himself. But once again he had the feeling that his curiosity wasn't purely professional. Now that he'd finally met her, his need to know everything about her was rapidly becoming a compulsion.

He'd expected her taste in lingerie to run to black lace and kinky cutouts so he was surprised to find that she preferred pastels and softly feminine designs. In spite of himself, his hand lingered caressingly on an ivory satin chemise that was the same color and texture as her skin.

Sharon came to a shocked standstill when she'd crossed the threshold of her bedroom and saw the man rummaging around in her drawer. His back was to her, but she could see his reflection in the dresser mirror. The way he was going through her intimate garments made her feel almost as naked and exposed as when he'd stripped her nightgown off her.

Her breath caught when she saw his hand move softly, erotically over the ivory chemise he was holding; it rushed out of her when he buried his face impulsively in the satiny folds and inhaled deeply.

"Just what . . . do you think . . . you're doing?" she demanded.

His head shot up and he saw her reflection in the mirror. For an instant, he looked like a kid who'd been caught with his hand in the cookie jar. "Sure smells good," he murmured with a self-conscious and rather appealing grin. "Feels good, too." Slowly, his eyes moved down her body as if he were picturing how she would look in the scrap of satin he was still holding possessively.

An uncontrollable shiver went through Sharon that had nothing to do with the cold, and her knuckles turned white from clutching the bath towel so tightly around her.

He frowned suddenly, as though confused and annoyed by his behavior and dropped his eyes. When he spoke, his tone was casual but very much under control. "But I don't think this would keep you very warm. None of these would." With a wave of his hand, he indicated the rest of her lingerie. The amber glow from the lamp on the night table slid and shimmered over the chemise as it slipped slowly, as if reluctantly, from his fingers into the drawer. "Don't you have anything warmer? Like a flannel night-gown?" He closed the drawer with one sure, hard motion. "I can't seem to find one."

"In the bottom drawer," Sharon told him, feeling better now that he'd explained his reason for being there. But his presence in her bedroom, no matter how honorable his intentions, was unnerving. "Never mind, I'll get it."

"I thought I'd told you to stay in the tub until I'd gotten you some warm clothes. What are you trying to do, catch pneumonia?" Before she'd taken more than a couple of steps into the room, he'd already found and pulled a flan-nel nightgown out of the bottom drawer and was carrying it over to her.

"Here, put this on," he ordered brusquely. Since her hands were busy holding the bath towel securely against her body, he slung the nightgown over her bare shoulder. "You'd better put a robe on too, and some slippers."

"Look, I'm perfectly capable of—"

"Hurry up before you catch a chill again," he said curtly as he brushed past her. "Come to the living room when you're ready. I've got a fire going," he added before he slammed his way out the door.

"Oh, what a . . . a . . ." Sharon was at a loss to find words to describe the man. Probably because she'd never met anyone like him. There was something dangerous about him, though she couldn't have said what it was. She sensed powerful emotions behind his carefully controlled facade, and an overpowering sexuality. She couldn't wait to get him out of her house.

Tossing her flannel nightgown to one side, she hurried over to the closet. Somehow, she needed to be fully dressed before she could confront him.

Three

Dressed in a bulky sweater, jeans, and ankle-high boots, Sharon strode purposefully into the living room a few minutes later to find Ross sitting cross-legged on the floor in front of the crackling fire, one hand wrapped comfortably around the coffee mug he was drinking from. The breath caught in her throat. He'd removed his wet shirt and left it hanging from the center of the mantelpiece. Firelight flickered over the lean, hard muscles of his shoulders and chest, and picked out the gold in his tawny hair.

The sight of him looking perfectly at home in her house would have been disturbing enough without his being half-naked; it added to Sharon's determination to get him out as quickly as possible.

A wry smile twisted his mouth when his eyes slid over her outfit, letting her know that he was aware of the real reason she'd needed to be fully dressed. "Feeling better?"

"Yes, I'm feeling fine now," she returned pointedly, "so you can—"

"Come on over to the fire and get some hot tea." Though he'd interrupted her, his tone was that of a solicitous host. With a polite nod, he indicated the brimming mug he'd left for her on the smoke-darkened brick hearth in front of the fire.

Sharon halted. It bothered her that he'd gone to all that trouble for her.

"It's good and hot and sure gets the chill out." As if in need of the heat radiating from his mug, he wrapped both hands around it before bringing it slowly to his lips.

In the blazing light from the fire, Sharon suddenly noticed that his lips had a bluish cast to them and his jeans were plastered to his body.

"You're still soaking wet," she cried accusingly. How could she throw him out when he was soaking wet?

He shrugged, unconcerned. "I'll be okay if I can just sit in front of the fire for a little bit."

Ross took another swallow of hot tea. Without seeming to, he watched the battle that was going on in her expressive brown eyes. She obviously couldn't wait to get rid of him, so why was she hesitating?

"Maybe you should—" Sharon stopped herself just as she was about to tell him to take off his jeans and let them dry in front of the fire also. But a closer look at the jeans clinging wetly to his long legs, emphasizing every sleekly toned muscle, made her realize that it wasn't such a good idea after all.

Turning, she hurried over to the sofa, and picking up the crocheted afghan that was draped over the back of it, she brought it over to him. "Why don't you put this around you? It's pure wool."

It was Ross's turn to be surprised by her thoughtful gesture. She obviously had intended to ask him to leave but seeing that he was still wet, had been unable to do so. He would never have expected a woman like her to be concerned with someone else's welfare.

"Don't worry about getting it wet," she urged. When he continued to hesitate, she bent over and wrapped the afghan around his shoulders and back, her hands soft as she draped the rest of it across his bare chest, letting it fall over his crossed legs.

Ross went rigid when he felt her fingers tuck one edge of the afghan under his armpit. Didn't she realize what she was doing to him or was she doing it deliberately? He slanted her a wary glance.

The expression on her face was one of total concentration. But there was a high spot of color on her cheeks that hadn't been there before, and she seemed to be having trouble tucking the other end of the afghan under his other armpit. He could have lifted his arm to make it easier for her but he didn't dare move so much as a muscle. He wasn't sure what he might do. He'd never been so aware of a woman in his life.

The scent of wildflowers wet with rain clung to her skin, filling his senses. Her luscious mouth was so close that he had only to lift his head to take it. He dropped his eyes—and saw the outline of her breasts through her sweater. The way she was bending over him, her breasts hung within easy reach of his hands like perfectly round, ripe fruit just waiting to be picked. His hands tightened around the mug.

"There," Sharon breathed with relief when she straightened up. "That should do it." She couldn't remember when so simple a task had been so difficult to perform. Her hands were shaking.

Ross's muttered thanks sounded more like a curse.

"You really shouldn't be sitting on that bare floor," Sharon said, trying to keep her tone polite but impersonal. She was grateful for the excuse to put some distance between them. Though he hadn't said a word or made a move while she was wrapping the afghan around him, the sexual tension between them had been almost palpable, deeply unsettling.

She couldn't remember the last time a man had affected her so intensely. As she walked over to one of the wicker armchairs flanking the fireplace, Sharon wondered whether he was aware of the sexuality he projected so effortlessly. Only once before had she been so strongly attracted to a man, although, as she had found out very early in her marriage, the raw sexuality that had made Buck a rock superstar was evident only when he was performing in front of an audience or high on cocaine.

With a deep sigh, Sharon pulled the loose cushions off one of the wicker chairs. She couldn't bear to think about the negative aspects of their marriage now that Buck was dead. Somehow it always added to her already overwhelming feelings of guilt. Carrying the cushions over to the fireplace, she resolutely pushed all thoughts of the past out of her mind. She was having enough trouble dealing with the present.

Sharon dropped the cushions side by side onto the pegged oak floor. "Try one of these. I'm sure it's warmer and more comfortable than the floor."

"But I'll get it all wet," he protested with the same look he'd given her when she'd offered him the afghan.

"That's all right. That's why I covered them in duck cloth." With her foot, she pushed the cushion that was nearest him right up against his thigh. "It's a very easy fabric to take care of."

He lifted his lean hips, allowing her to slide the thick, foam rubber pillow under him. "*You* covered them?"

She wondered why he found that so amazing. "Yes."

As if he still found that difficult to believe, Ross stared intently at the armchair on his right. No wonder he hadn't recognized the old wicker chairs. For as long as he could remember they had been painted white and covered with fashionably thin, flowery chintz cushions. Now the wicker frames were a warm golden tone, and thick, cream-colored pillows made the armchairs seem twice their size and twice as inviting.

He could feel her watching him, probably wondering why he was staring at the chair so intently. "You don't usually see wicker in its natural state these days," he said by way of explanation.

"I know." She laughed softly as she sank down onto the cushion next to his. "I had to peel layers and layers of white paint off them to get them back to their natural color."

"You did that, too?"

"Yes, it's a hobby of mine." Sharon was relieved that their conversation was taking an impersonal turn, but there was something about his attitude that she found disturbing even though she couldn't have said what it was. "I enjoy making slipcovers and drapes," she went on, "and restoring old furniture and..." She shrugged self-consciously and reached for her tea. "Things like that."

The more he knew about her, Ross noted resentfully, the less she fit the image of her he'd created in his mind. Turning his head, he slowly scanned the living room to take in the rest of her "improvements."

The sofa wasn't new either, as he'd initially thought, but had been skillfully reupholstered in the same cream-colored fabric, and piles of pillows had been added to allow the sitter to customize the sofa for his or her comfort. The cool fabric and neutral colors, the warm, golden touches of natural wicker made for a comfortable yet understatedly elegant look. A profusion of potted and hanging plants added to the outdoor, summery feeling of the decor.

She'd certainly done a great job on the old place, Ross was forced to admit. She'd managed to turn a house that had always lacked warmth into a home any man would look forward to coming back to at the end of the day. He was becoming more intrigued by her every minute. He turned back to her with a smile that held more admiration than he'd intended. "You're a very creative lady." His eyes locked with hers, and he found himself wondering how creative she was in...other areas. "You can decorate my place any time."

His searching gaze, the deep caressing rumble of his voice created an intimacy between them that took Sharon totally by surprise. Tearing her eyes away, she took several gulps of tea without tasting it.

"I'm Ross Baxter, by the way," he said casually, offering his hand.

"Sharon Farrell." Since she was holding the mug in her right hand, and was still too rattled to be able to think quickly enough to switch it, Sharon returned his handshake with her left hand. She'd only meant to touch fingers with him, anyway, but his hand swallowed up hers.

"Farrell?" Ross repeated, making a mental note of the fact that she was using her maiden name.

"That's right." Why did she have the feeling that he was making fun of her? Just as she was about to free her hand from the disturbingly strong, warm crush of his, he tightened his hold on her, turning her hand so that firelight bounced off her gold wedding band, making it gleam.

Ross found it rather ironic that she would still be wearing the wedding ring of the man she'd killed. He'd have thought that particular piece of jewelry would be the first thing she would have gotten rid of in her quest for a new identity. "And where's *Mr.* Farrell?"

Her hand went limp in his and she swallowed convulsively. "My husband is...dead."

"I'm sorry." Ross wasn't lying. She didn't know how sorry he was, but she'd soon find out. He released her hand. "What happened?"

"It was an...an accident," she stammered, gripping the mug with both hands as though she needed to hold on to something.

He was surprised by the intensity of her reaction, and had to warn himself against being taken in by her expert playacting. "That must have been pretty tough on you. I know what it's like to lose someone you love unexpectedly." Wondering what her story would be, he leaned toward her. "How did it happen?"

Sharon was unable to decide which bothered her more: his blunt question or his disturbing closeness. She had no intention of putting up with either and pulled back. "Mr. Baxter, I—"

"I think we can dispense with the formalities after what we've been through tonight, don't you?" An ironic smile played on his lips, reminding her that he'd held her naked in his arms.

"Look, Mr. Baxter, I don't mean to be rude," Sharon said rudely, "but what were you doing on my property?"

He laughed. "I'm afraid you've got it all wrong, *Mrs. Farrell*. *You* were the one who was trespassing on *my* property."

"What?"

"You see that row of pine trees out there?" He turned and pointed through the side window. "That marks the boundary between your property and mine. The pier that goes with your house is way over there on the right." He swung his arm past the large picture window that fronted the house, all the way over to the other side window. The shadowy outline of a pier was visible in the hazy moonlight. "The one you took a dive off belongs to the cabin—my place."

"I'd assumed that cabin was part of this property. No one told me otherwise."

"It was once," he allowed smoothly. "The cabin used to be the guest house, but after the original owner died the property was split up. I bought the cabin as a summer place a couple of years ago."

"But I was assured that my closest neighbor lived over a mile from here," Sharon blurted out, "or I would never have—" She stopped herself, but not in time.

"Moved in here?" he finished for her. "Don't tell me that you're hiding out, too?"

"No!" Sharon gasped when she got her voice back.

"Well, I am." With a heavy sigh, he set his empty mug down on the hearth. "And, now, it's my turn to be rude. I'm not exactly thrilled to find that someone has moved into this house either. I was hoping to have this usually deserted stretch of country all to myself this summer." He tugged the afghan around him with a nervous, somewhat irritated gesture. "Seems I've got a slight case of burnout, so my doctor ordered total peace and quiet for the next few months." He frowned. "My chances for that don't look so good any more."

"Well, I moved in here hoping to find some peace and quiet myself," Sharon returned defensively, "so I certainly wouldn't do anything to disturb yours."

"You mean, like tonight?" he drawled, making his trace of a Southern accent more pronounced. "Is that what you consider peace and quiet, taking a dive off the deep end of a pier?"

"I did not take a dive off a pier! I told you, I just went for a walk because I was having trouble sleeping," Sharon shot back, slamming her mug down on the hearth next to his. "If you hadn't come screaming out of the darkness, I would never have lost my balance and fallen into the water in the first place!"

"Okay, don't get your feathers ruffled," he murmured soothingly. "I guess it was my fault at that. But why were you having trouble sleeping?"

That was the second time that evening he'd asked her that question, and the same warning bell went off in Sharon's head. She sat up stiffly and faced him head-on. "How much do you want for the cabin?"

He stared at her incredulously for a moment. She felt a definite sense of satisfaction at having succeeded in rattling him for a change.

"Do I understand you correctly? Are you offering to buy my cabin?"

"That's right. I'm willing to pay top dollar."

"You sure do value your privacy, don't you?" He shrugged off the afghan as if he suddenly found it too constricting. Firelight slid over the smooth, hard muscles of his shoulders and chest. "But I just got here. I haven't even unpacked yet," he added with a charming grin.

A bit too charming, Sharon decided. She knew she was acting impulsively but her instinct told her to stay as far away from this man as possible. She'd never been very smart when it came to money so she didn't care if she took a loss. It was worth any amount of money to her to keep more trouble out of her life. And this man, she felt sure, would be nothing but trouble. "You may not have to," she said coldly. "Name your price."

A bitter rage twisted inside Ross and it was all he could do to hold it in. He should have known she was the type of person who thought she could buy anything or anybody. Why was he so surprised? She'd probably bought her way out of a murder indictment.

He took a long, steadying breath and warned himself against letting his emotions get the better of him. In order to win her confidence and get her to expose herself, he was going to have play *his* part as ruthlessly as *she* played with people to get what she wanted.

"Sorry, no sale," he told her flat out. "You see, I bought the cabin as an anniversary present for my wife." He paused deliberately. "Though I wish now I'd never set eyes on the place."

Sharon wondered at the bitterness in his tone. "Why?" she blurted out before she could stop herself. It bothered her that she was curious about his marital status. "Are you divorced now?"

"No." He ran his fingers through the tawny tangle of his hair and stared down at the floor. "My wife was murdered in that cabin. Shot to death."

Her sharp intake of breath was more than he'd hoped for, and when he looked up at her he saw that her face had gone white.

She exhaled raggedly. "That's awful. How did it happen?"

"From the evidence, the police are pretty sure it was a burglar." Turning away, Ross stared into the fire. It surprised and annoyed him that he was unable to lie to her face. But then, he'd never been a good liar. He'd made it his life's work to expose liars and cheats, the corrupters and destroyers of this world. But it galled him whenever he was forced to use their methods to trap them.

Sharon could see how difficult it was for him to talk about the tragedy. She knew the feeling only too well so she didn't press him for the details. She just wished there was something she could do to help him.

"My wife came out here by herself that weekend," he went on, seemingly compelled to do so. "I had to stay in Baltimore to finish up some work. I was supposed to join her on Sunday but someone broke into the house Saturday night and..." He stopped as though unable to continue. He could feel her listening to him intently, barely breathing. "She was already dead when I found her... lying in a pool of blood."

"Oh, my God," Sharon murmured brokenly. From her own experience she knew what an ordeal that must have been and she hurt for him.

"I still can't forget it though it happened over two years ago and I've worked myself to the brink of a nervous collapse trying. I haven't been able to set foot in that cabin since." A labored sigh escaped him. "Until tonight. Coming back here was my doctor's idea." He looked over at her then, his eyes intense. "He says it's time I stopped running away and finally faced what happened."

"That's easy for him to say," she muttered bitterly, on the defensive again. "The place isn't filled with unbearable memories for him."

"True, but if I've learned one thing these last two years, it's that running away doesn't solve anything either." He leaned toward her, and Sharon found herself being caught and held by eyes the same startling shade of amber as her dead husband's. She felt that he could see right through her. "You can leave a place behind but you carry the memories with you wherever you go."

"That's . . . true," Sharon admitted reluctantly, looking away.

He leaned closer still, his warm breath brushing her face when he spoke, his words reverberating inside her. "You see, Doc's got this theory that unless you face up to what happened, you'll never find lasting peace."

"Peace," she repeated softly. She sounded as if she couldn't remember what that was or as if she'd given up hope of ever finding it again.

And Ross knew that he'd hooked her. "I think the worst part of it is the guilt."

"Yes," she breathed, staring into space. "Guilt and . . . and not being able to bring them back."

Ross was stunned by the despair tightening her voice, twisting in the dark depths of her eyes. Even a phony like her couldn't be that good an actress. He watched as she managed to get herself under control.

"But why should *you* feel guilty?" she asked, her voice warm now and full of concern for him. "You weren't to blame."

Ross hesitated, but it wasn't deliberate this time. His last meeting with Buck flashed into his mind. He'd sworn to himself that he wouldn't let personal feelings interfere with his job, but there was nothing he could do about it. "I should have been there," he bit out the words, guilt and anger knotting up his insides. "I'm sure I would have been able to stop it from happening. If only I'd—"

"No! No, don't do that to yourself!" Sharon broke in, her face mirroring the anguish on his. Wanting to let him know that someone else understood what he was going through, she placed her hand on his arm. He tensed at her touch. "I know how you feel. We all feel responsible when something terrible happens to someone we love...but things happen sometimes that are completely out of our control and..."

Tears lumped in Sharon's throat and flooded her eyes as she relived the moment when the gun had gone off and she'd watched with horror and disbelief as Buck crumbled up in pain before her. The tears spilled down her face.

Ross stared at her in amazement. She covered her face with both hands as if trying to hold back the tears and muffle the sobs shaking her delicate body. Before he realized what he was doing he reached out and gathered her up in his arms.

Sharon gasped with surprise when she felt his arms go around her, the achingly tender way that he was holding her. Vaguely, she realized what she was allowing him to do and that the man was a perfect stranger. But it had been so long since she'd known tenderness or had felt someone's arms around her, and she knew that this man understood what she was going through because he'd been there himself. She felt closer to him at that moment than she had to anyone in years.

Letting go of what little there was left of her control, she let her body sink against his and her head fell onto his shoulder. Gripping his sides with both hands, she clung to him as the reaction to the physical and emotional traumas she'd been going through that evening finally overwhelmed her.

Ross stiffened when he felt her body melt against his. The way she was clinging to him made his pulse quicken. He tried not to be aware of her physically but with every sob her soft breasts shuddered against his chest, sending his blood pounding through him. It took every shred of willpower he possessed to stop himself from becoming fully aroused.

Taken in by her tears, he'd forgotten who she was for a moment—but only for a moment. He continued to hold her, trying not to feel her. In self-defense, he willed his mind to be detached, even ruthless. She was closer to the breaking point than he'd realized. It shouldn't take him long to break her down completely and get the proof he needed to convict her. If only she didn't feel so good in his arms.

As the pain and guilt drained out of her and her tears began to subside, Sharon became aware of the bare muscular shoulder cushioning her head, the lean hard wall of his chest crushing her breasts. Her head lay nestled in the crook of his shoulder, the pulse that beat strong and hard in his throat vibrating against her parted lips. The musky scent of his skin swirled around her senses. She could feel his body heat through her clothes, could feel her own body beginning to heat under it.

She pushed against his sides and felt sleek muscles contract under her hands just before she pulled away from him.

They stared at one another for a long moment while the hiss and crackle of logs being consumed by fire provided the only sound in the room as they both held their breaths. Though she tried, Sharon was unable to break the connection between them. His eyes were like molten gold in the firelight, but they were burning with an inner heat, and she knew that he was experiencing the same sensual pull on his senses that she was.

Dropping her eyes, Sharon noticed the spot on his shoulder that was wet with her tears. "Looks like I got you wet again," she joked feebly in an attempt to lessen the sexual tension still vibrating between them. "Sorry."

"Don't worry about it," he said, his voice tight.

"I guess my nerves are shot from not sleeping," she rattled on, wiping her tear-stained cheeks with trembling hands. She hoped he couldn't see how flushed she was. "And from the dunking in the cold water and...and everything."

"You must be exhausted."

"Yes." A ragged sigh escaped her. She hadn't realized how tired she was. "Yes, I am."

"I'd better get going then." With one lithe motion, he was on his feet. "Why don't you go to bed now?"

"No, I'd rather sleep out here." Reaching for the cushion he'd been sitting on, she slid it up against hers.

"I'll put some more logs on the fire then."

"Thanks."

Quickly, Ross built up the fire so that it would last until morning. He was grateful for the distraction. By the time he'd finished getting his shirt on, he was in control again. When he turned back to her, she was lying across the pillows, her legs tucked under her. She was so petite, her whole body fit on the makeshift mattress except for her feet, which hung over the edge. She was having trouble keeping her eyes open.

Bending over, Ross retrieved the afghan and covered Sharon with it. Before he could straighten up, she reached up and grabbed his hand.

"Are you going to be all right?" she asked with a worried glance in the direction of the cabin.

For a moment, Ross was too thrown to respond. "Sure," he said stiffly, pulling his hand away. "I'll be fine."

"I hope so," she murmured thickly as her eyelids began to close.

Ross stood there as if nailed to the spot. She looked so small and lost huddled under the blanket. Her eyelashes were still wet with tears and her lips were parted, soft and vulnerable. No, she certainly didn't look like a murderess.

With a silent curse, Ross turned and walked over to the door. He'd seen enough murderers in his time to know that some of them didn't look the part, and that *they* were the ones you really had to watch out for. Now that he'd finally met her, he could understand how she'd managed to fool Buck, the police, even the court of inquiry.

But she wasn't going to fool him, Ross promised himself as he closed the door quietly behind him.

Four

Sharon took a leisurely sip of coffee, not because she meant to savor it, but because she knew that once she'd drained the mug she could no longer put off the inevitable moment when she'd have to go outside. She'd dawdled so long over breakfast—brunch, actually, since it was almost two in the afternoon—that her eggs and toast were cold by the time she'd finished them. Now her coffee was lukewarm. She hated lukewarm coffee.

She made a face as she took another slow sip and continued staring out the open kitchen window. It was a bright, cloudless day but one more suited to April than June. The sun gave off light without heat. The powerful wind that had shaken the trees and rattled the windowpanes last night was gone; not so much as a breeze remained. In the cool, crisp light everything stood out sharply: the gnarled pine trees, the cabin nestling among them across the way, each rock in the man-made barrier at the foot of the embankment.

Even the tall, lanky figure of the man standing at the end of the pier, legs wide apart, hands sunk deep into the back pockets of his jeans seemed in sharp focus as he stared intently down at the narrow, winding ribbon of river.

The surface of the water was mirror smooth, a pale-blue reflection of the sky above, giving no hint of the treacherous currents below. A strange stillness hung in the air as if life were suspended, waiting for something to happen. Or so it seemed to Sharon. She was still unable to shake off the sense of unreality that had gripped her the moment she woke up.

Although her sleep had been deep and mercifully dreamless, it had taken her several minutes to remember why she was sleeping on the floor in front of the fireplace instead of in bed. When she did remember, there had actually been a moment when she wondered whether it had all been a dream. The sight of the two empty coffee mugs on the smoke-darkened hearth assured her it hadn't.

But the full force of what had happened the night before didn't hit her until she was running the water for her bath. Not only had a total stranger seen her naked but she'd broken down and cried in his arms like a child. She'd clung to him, eager for the feel of his arms around her. She'd never known such tenderness and warmth; somehow, it had all seemed so natural last night. But in the cool, clear light of day all she felt was a deep sense of shame and a kind of fearful resentment toward him because he'd seen her at her most vulnerable. She didn't know how she would ever be able to face him again.

Sharon suddenly realized why she was taking forever to finish her coffee.

With a sigh of irritation, she poured what was left down the drain. As she quickly washed the mug she reminded herself that if she wasted any more time she'd be late for her appointment. She was glad that she'd be spending the rest of the afternoon in Baltimore. Impulsively, she decided to take in the sights while she was at it, and stay over for dinner, maybe take in a movie—a double feature.

After quickly drying her hands, Sharon pulled her suit jacket off the back of the chair and slipped it on. Grabbing her shoulder bag off the table, she hurried down the hall to the other entrance to the house; the one facing the woods.

Since she'd been too busy fixing up the house the last few weeks to find time to clean out the garage, which was as filled with old family possessions as an attic, she'd been forced to park her car in the driveway.

Sharon halted abruptly when she reached the corner of the house. The driveway ran parallel to the row of pine trees separating the house from the cabin so she knew that her sports car was visible from the pier. Carefully, and with a full measure of self-disgust at her cowardice, she peered around the corner. Ross was bending over the end of the pier, his back to her, pulling some kind of contraption up out of the water.

Car keys in hand, Sharon tiptoed over to the classic Jaguar convertible, gravel crunching under her shoes like broken glass. A nervous glance at Ross told her that he was either too far away to hear the excruciating noise or it sounded that way only to her. With a sigh of relief, she opened the car door and slid behind the wheel. Deciding to wait until she was on the road to get the map she'd need out of the glove compartment, she quickly slipped the key in the ignition and turned it. Nothing happened.

Pumping the gas pedal, she tried again and again, cringing inside at the horrible, tearing noise the engine made as it protested her increasingly frantic efforts to get it to turn over. Through the windshield she saw Ross straighten up and look over his shoulder at her.

"Damn," she muttered under her breath. She was sure that now that he'd seen her, he'd come over; she proceeded to strip the gears. But he merely waved at her in the most neighborly fashion and went back to what he was doing.

Ross finished baiting the crab trap, trying to look more involved than he actually was. He knew that no matter how hard she tried, Sharon would be unable to get her car started with the rotor missing. The rotor, which he'd removed from the engine last night after she'd gone to sleep for the first time, was in his tool box. Since he could fix an engine as well as most mechanics, he'd thought it a clever way to get to meet her. If he'd known she was going to fall off the end of his pier, he wouldn't have bothered. He'd meant to put the rotor back the first safe chance he got. He hadn't counted on her using the car today.

For a moment he was tempted to go over and offer his help, but for some reason, he wanted her to come to him, to need him as she had last night. Something quickened inside him when he remembered how she'd felt in his arms. He gave the trap a savage tug.

Sharon checked her wristwatch: ten after two. Her appointment was for three-thirty and Baltimore was an hour and a half drive from St. Michaels. She didn't even know where the nearest mechanic was located.

"Come on, baby," she murmured soothingly. "You can do it." She gave the Jaguar a reassuring pat on the dashboard before giving the ignition another try. The motor sputtered and choked out another protest but wouldn't budge. "If you keep this up, I'm going to trade you in on a new car, so help me." She pumped the gas pedal impatiently. "I really mean it this time." The '53 Jag ignored her threats. It let out the metallic equivalent of a high-pitched scream, shuddered once, and went dead.

As casually as possible, Ross turned the chicken wire and wood trap around so he'd be facing Sharon when she called him for help with her car. So he was surprised to see her get out of the car, and without so much as a glance in his direction, walk resolutely over to the grilled hood. Bending down, she lifted and secured it with one expert motion.

A wry smile of admiration flickered across his face as he watched her check the battery, the oil, and the water level in the radiator. He'd misjudged her again: she obviously wasn't used to asking a man for help. He was glad that he'd set it up so she would have to.

It suddenly occurred to him that she might know more about car engines than he'd realized—anyone who drove a classic car and kept it in such mint condition didn't think of cars as mere transportation—though she'd have to be an expert to find the missing part.

He couldn't afford to take any chances.

Getting to his feet, Ross called over to her, "Having trouble with your car?"

"Yes," she called back, her tone exasperated.

"I'm pretty good with cars. Maybe I can help." Quickly, he covered the length of the pier and started up the embankment toward her.

Sharon wiped her hands on the clean rag she always kept under the bucket seat while she watched Ross climb the grassy slope moving with easy grace and power. Suddenly, she reexperienced the sensation of being cradled securely in his arms as he carried her up the embankment the night before. When she put the rag down on the fender, her hand was unsteady.

"Hi." He flashed her a devastating smile when he came to a halt beside her that took Sharon totally by surprise.

"Hello," she managed airily, turning away from him to look down at the motor as if she could actually see what she was looking at.

Ross hadn't expected such a cool reception from her after last night, and it bothered him. He was surprised by her outfit as well; it wasn't the kind of thing someone who'd been part of the flashy world of hard rock would wear.

She looked every bit the cool, efficient businesswoman today in her tailored gray flannel suit, her black alligator shoulder bag a stylish version of an attaché case. The sharp masculine cut of the suit was softened by a pearl-gray silk blouse and the undeniably feminine curves it was unable to disguise. High heels added three inches to her height, bringing the top of her head to his shoulder; taupe hose gave her legs a smoky sheen.

"Do you know anything about motors?" she asked without looking at him. Her tone was so impersonal that he might have been a mechanic she was considering hiring.

It irritated the hell out of him.

"I've already checked the battery and—"

"How are you, Sharon?"

Startled, Sharon looked up at Ross. It was the first time he'd called her by name, his deep voice and soft Southern drawl adding to the intimacy of his tone.

"What?"

"How are you?" Ross repeated with an easy grin that belied his determination to stop her from treating him like a stranger. "Feeling any aftereffects from last night?"

"No, I'm fine." The carefree wave of her hand sought to dismiss the subject entirely. The last thing she wanted was to talk about last night. "It's my car. I can't get it to—"

"Did you sleep all right?" he persisted, sunlight picking out the strands of gold buried in his tawny hair just as the firelight had the night before. Intense amber eyes locked with hers and everything that had happened last night came alive between them.

"Yes, very well," Sharon heard herself say. Though she tried, she was unable to break the strange hold he had on her. She had the feeling that this man had the power to see right through her, to make her say or do anything he wanted. This must be what it's like to be hypnotized, she thought.

Ross saw confusion mingle first with apprehension then with a kind of fascination in the dark expressive depths of Sharon's eyes. Her lips parted unconsciously, soft and vulnerable and very inviting. His own lips parted in response.

Drawing in an unsteady breath, Sharon turned away and looked down at the motor. Tiny dots danced in front of her eyes as though she'd been staring at the sun too long. "Look, I've got to get this car started."

Her manner was cool, impersonal once more. But it was merely a facade, Ross noted with satisfaction, a defense against him. He was getting to her, though he didn't know why—any more than he knew why she got to him. He turned his attention to the car. "What seems to be the trouble?"

"I can't get it to start."

"She sure is a beauty." Admiration glowed in his eyes as he took in the long, elegant lines of the snow-white Jaguar convertible. "1953 XK 120. One of the classiest sports cars ever made."

Sharon was amazed that he would recognize the year and model of her car. He was the most extraordinary man, she thought irritably. Slowly, almost sensuously, he ran his hand over the front fender's long, swooping curves. She felt a tiny shiver go up her spine, which increased her irritation. She wanted him to fix her car, not make love to it.

"Are you sure you know how to fix it?" she demanded defensively.

A slow smile curved his lips. "Positive."

"I don't mean to rush you, but I've got a very important appointment and . . ." She glanced at her wristwatch. "Oh, my God, I'm late already. How long do you think it'll take?"

"That all depends," Ross said evasively. He knew it would take him less than ten minutes to replace the rotor he'd removed from her car but the chance to spend some time with her was too good to resist. "If you're worried about being late for your appointment, I can drive you to town in my car. I'll work on the engine when we get back."

"But I'm not going into town. My appointment is in Baltimore."

"Baltimore?" He just managed to conceal his surprise. He thought she didn't know anyone in Baltimore. "I wondered why you were all gussied up," he teased. "Got a heavy date, huh?"

"No, I don't have a date," she shot back impatiently. "I have a very important business meeting that I can't postpone because the—" She stopped herself just in time; in another second she might have given herself away. She sighed with frustration. "Is there a bus I can take?"

"Forget about *that* idea," he told her emphatically. "You need a car just to drive to the bus station. *I'll* drive you to

Baltimore and when you're through with your meeting I'll drive you back.''

"I couldn't let you do that.'' She knew that it was the only sensible solution to her problem but the prospect of spending several hours in his company unnerved her.

"Why not?'' He shrugged matter-of-factly. "I'd planned on driving up tomorrow to take care of some unfinished business of my own. I'll take care of it today instead.''

Anxiously, Sharon glanced at her watch and tried to think of a logical excuse for not letting him drive her. There was no logical excuse.

"Come on,'' he urged, "the longer we stand here talking about it, the later you're going to be.''

"All right,'' she agreed reluctantly. Her appointment was too important to miss. "Just let me make a fast call to let them know I'm going to be a few minutes late.''

"I'll bring my car around,'' he tossed over his shoulder, already on his way.

When Sharon came back outside, not only was his car already idling in her driveway but he'd managed to change from his T-shirt and jeans into a turtleneck sweater and corduroy pants; a tweed jacket with suede patches was slung over the back of the seat.

He looked up at her from behind the wheel. "Did you have any trouble?''

"No, it just took forever to track down the person I have the—'' She stopped, drawing in an astonished breath, as she finally noticed his car. "Isn't that the first model Corvette ever made?''

He nodded and watched her reaction as if he'd been anticipating it.

Eyes wide with excitement, Sharon admired the long, sleek lines of the gleaming black sports car; the idling motor sounded like a low, warning purr. "Oh, it's gorgeous!"

Ross watched the excitement light up Sharon's face. It snagged at something inside him. "After seeing your car," he murmured wryly, "I thought you might appreciate it." Reaching across the red leather bucket seat, he pushed down the handle and swung the door open for her. "Looks like we've got something in common."

The ironic smile that tugged at the corners of his mouth made it clear that he was as amazed by that as she was.

"What a lovely section this is," Sharon said, admiring the quaint, port-side neighborhood tucked away from the glass-and-steel downtown area of Baltimore. Beautifully preserved Federal town houses, each one different from the next, stood in snaggletoothed rows, none of them higher than three stories, all of them looking freshly painted in a riot of pastels.

"This is Fells Point," Ross informed Sharon while he executed a right turn on to one of the narrow cobblestone streets. "Most of these houses date back to the early 1700s. As you can see from all the antique shops and art galleries, Fells Point is the Greenwich Village of Baltimore." Wondering what kind of business she could be transacting in a section of the city where artists primarily lived and worked, he shot her a questioning look. "You did say Lancaster Street?"

"Yes, Lancaster."

"Well, this is Lancaster," he said, bringing the car to a smooth stop at the red light. "What number?"

Sharon hesitated. She suddenly realized that she couldn't risk letting him know where she was going. "*This* is Lancaster Street?'' she asked, trying to keep her tone matter-of-fact.

"That's right."

"Then I'll get out here." Bending over, she quickly retrieved her combination attaché and pocketbook from the carpeted floor of the car and slung it over her shoulder. "It's only a couple of doors down."

Ross gave her a long look. How could she know exactly where the building was when she hadn't even known where the street was? She obviously didn't want him to know where she was going.

"I insist on dropping you off at the door," he told her, forcing a teasing smile. "This is a first-rate limousine service. We guarantee door-to-door service."

"No, this is fine, really," Sharon insisted. She knew that she was being overly cautious but she'd been too trusting in the past and had always regretted it. "Thanks for everything." Sending him a quick, grateful smile, she grabbed the door handle just as the traffic light turned green.

"Hey, hold it," Ross called out. "Let me get over to the curb." Shifting, he drove to the far corner, pulling into the empty space in front of a fire hydrant. He left the motor running and turned to face her. "What time do you want me to pick you up?"

"That's not necessary," Sharon said as she started to get out of the car again. "I'll get a bus back."

Sitting up, he reached over and grabbed her arm, holding her back. Sharon stiffened as she felt the heat of his hand right through her jacket. "There are no buses to St. Michaels, only to Easton. When you get there, you're going to have to find some other means of transportation home, you know."

No, she didn't know. "I just didn't want to put you to any more trouble than I already have," she murmured, pulling her arm away.

"It's no trouble." An appealing grin softened the stark lines of his face and made tiny crinkles at the corners of his golden eyes. "I have to drive back to St. Michaels anyway." He leaned toward her and she caught a whiff of that musky scent that had clung, mingling with her scent, to the towel last night. "So what time shall I pick you up?"

Sharon pulled back. "I . . . I don't know." She looked at her watch and had to force her mind to concentrate on what she was doing. "It's a quarter to four now. My meeting should take at least an hour." She looked over at him. "Let's make it five-fifteen, just to be sure."

"Five-fifteen it is." He sank back against the bucket seat. "What's the address again?"

"The address?" Sharon repeated. Stalling for thinking time, she dug into the outside pouch of her attaché. "Do you remember that brick plaza we passed a couple of streets back . . . the one that looks out on the waterfront?"

"Sure."

"Why don't we meet there?"

"The waterfront plaza?"

Sharon heard the surprise in his voice. "Yes." Having found the sunglasses she was searching for, she quickly slipped them on. "Just in case I, uhh...finish up earlier than expected," she attempted to explain, "I'd like to look around a bit."

Ross suppressed a sardonic smile. He would have expected someone like her to be a good liar. So she didn't want him to know where she was going. He wondered why.

Her eyes concealed by the sunglasses, Sharon was finally able to look over at Ross. "Is that all right?"

He got out of the car without answering her. In a few long-legged strides he was at her door. After checking the oncoming traffic to make sure that it was safe for her to get out of the car, he opened the door.

She looked startled for a moment as though she wasn't accustomed to men behaving courteously.

"I told you this was a first-class limousine service," he teased, offering his hand to help her out.

The hand that swallowed up hers was warm and moist and brought up deeply unsettling memories of the night before.

"Five-fifteen, the waterfront plaza," he said. "It's a date." Ross felt Sharon's hand tense in his at the word "date," then she pulled her hand away abruptly.

"I really have to go. I'm already late for my appointment," she said as if she wanted him to think that was the reason for her reaction. With a nervous gesture, she pushed the huge sunglasses up against the bridge of her nose.

Ross was sure that she was wearing the sunglasses as a precaution against anyone recognizing her. What she obviously didn't realize was that once someone had seen that incredible mouth of hers, he wasn't likely to forget it. He watched as she crossed over to the sidewalk, trying not to notice the soft, feminine sway of her hips, the perfect line of her calves through the smoky sheen of her stockings.

Leaving the motor idling, Ross went over to the trunk of his car. From where he'd parked on the corner he had an unobstructed view of Lancaster Street. Bending over, he opened the trunk and started rummaging around inside just in case she might look back to see if he was still there. Out of the corner of his eye, he watched her check the numbers on the doors of the buildings against the calling card she was holding.

He picked up the box containing the roll of film he'd shot on her last night and slipped it into his pocket. As he was reaching for the manila envelope he'd stashed there earlier he saw her go into a building; the fifth one from the corner. Ross made a note of that on the flap of the envelope after he'd slammed the trunk shut and slid behind the wheel.

He was tempted to drive around the block and check out the building but he knew that he only had an hour and a half to take care of his own business and get back. Tossing the manila envelope onto the seat next to him, he shifted into first and pulled away from the curb.

Five

Moving the manila envelope to his left hand, Ross pushed his way through the glass doors bearing the bright gold legend, The Baltimore Examiner, Circulation over 1,260,000. With the exception of a young man studying the prize-winning news photos lining one rosewood-paneled wall, a large black portfolio clutched nervously in one hand, the ultramodern reception room was empty of visitors.

His shoes sinking soundlessly into the plush beige carpet, Ross made his way over to the reception desk that was strewn with incoming and outgoing packages. The pretty young receptionist was busy talking animatedly on the phone, a copy of a fashion magazine spread out before her. Irritation flashed in her hazel eyes; she clearly resented being interrupted in the middle of a personal call.

"Oh, it's *you*," she purred when she finally deigned to look up at him. She twirled a lock of streaked blond hair around one finger and literally batted her eyelashes at him. Like many a twenty-year-old trying to look older and more sophisticated, she wore far too much makeup.

"I have to go now, Cindy," she said abruptly into the phone. "I'll call you right back." She hung up, ignoring the lights that were flashing wildly all over the computerized intercom system. "Well, if it isn't R.B. Huntley in the flesh."

"Hi, Debbie. Any messages?"

"Where have you been keeping yourself, stranger?" Without looking, she reached automatically into one of the many built-in slots in the circular rosewood cubicle surrounding her. "Out on another one of your mysterious assignments?"

"Something like that," Ross said, accepting the pile of telephone-message slips she was handing him. "Is Sam available?"

"I wouldn't know," she returned with a flirtatious smile. Picking up the receiver, she pushed the appropriate button. "But *I* am."

"*Now* you tell me," he joshed, "just as I'm about to go out on the field again."

"I've told you plenty of..." She paused and her voice and manner underwent a complete transformation. "Mr. Huntley is here to see you." She couldn't have sounded more efficient. "Yes, he's here in person." There was a pause as she listened to the party on the other end. "Fine. I'll tell him." She hung up with a wistful sigh. "You can go right in, R.B."

"Thanks, Debbie." He gave her a polite smile and started toward the hall. "See you later."

"I only wish," Debbie muttered under her breath. With another sigh, she began to answer one of the flashing calls.

Slipping the manila envelope under one arm, Ross quickly flipped through the pile of phone messages while he walked down the long carpeted hallway. Without looking up, he made a sharp right to where the offices of the *Sunday Magazine* section were located. Stacking the messages in descending order of importance, he strode through the huge copy room that was alive with activity, the constant, overlapping ringing of phones and word processors flashing on all sides.

He came to a halt in front of the glass-and-rosewood-enclosed office that stood like a square island in the center of the room. The door with its brass nameplate, S. Carson—Editor, was ajar. Slipping the messages into his pocket, Ross let himself in and closed the door behind him. "Hi, Sam."

Samantha Carson looked up from the photo layouts she'd been examining with cool gray eyes. In her mid-fifties, she had the slim, boyish figure and boundless energy of a young girl. She always reminded Ross of a highly strung thoroughbred racehorse. She wore her ash-blond hair pulled back into a French twist, which emphasized her patrician bone structure and the sharp lines of her nose and lips. With her Chanel-style suit and a rope of pearls, she looked the picture of timeless elegance.

"I thought you were coming by *tomorrow*," she snapped as though his being there now upset all her plans.

Ross smiled. He was one of the few people who worked for *The Examiner* who wasn't put off by Sam's sharp tongue. He knew that she was a perfectionist who demanded and got the best out of her people. Like him, she'd made journalism her life and she was one of the few people Ross respected and admired unconditionally.

Sam was the one who'd made it possible for Ross to get into investigative reporting, and he knew he could always count on her to back him up when things got tough. Once she believed in a story, no matter how controversial, she fought for it for all she was worth. The result had been a Pulitzer prize for Ross for his piece on drug pushers preying on elementary school children.

He started over to the desk piled high with stacks of papers and layouts; in the six years he'd worked for her he'd yet to see the top of her desk. "I know I told you I'd stop by tomorrow, Sam, but—"

"Did you bring the Libby Holman copy?" she interrupted impatiently.

"Here it is." Stopping in front of her desk, Ross waved the manila envelope.

She held out an imperious hand. "Hand it over." A frown creased her high brow as she waited for him to finish tearing off the corner of the flap and put it in his pocket. She was used to his habit of jotting things down on envelopes, cocktail napkins or inside matchbook covers so she didn't question it. She merely grabbed the envelope avidly. "How is it?"

"I think it's good," Ross admitted simply.

"Hmm," she said. It was one of her *I'll*-decide-that hmms. Pulling the typewritten pages out of the manila envelope, she quickly scanned the lead. A thin, arched eyebrow went up and he knew that she liked it. "Not bad." Coming from her that was a high compliment. She dropped the pages on top of her must-be-read-immediately stack and sat back in her suede swivel chair. "How was your trip to New York? Did you turn up anything new on the Libby Holman case?"

"A couple of things."

"Like what?" She sat up again, a spark of interest in her eyes as she reached for a cigarette.

"I thought you stopped smoking, Sam," Ross said disapprovingly as he watched her light up.

"I did. But I started again." With an impatient hand she waved away his complaint as well as the smoke she'd exhaled. "So tell me, what did you find?"

"Nothing to stop the presses about. I still can't prove conclusively that she killed her husband—"

"Well, no one expected you to," she interrupted again. "It happened over fifty years ago."

"But I think I've got a new angle on the story. And I've got something else for you." Digging into his pocket, Ross took out the roll of film and placed it on the desk in front of her. "Give this to Eddie Marshall to process, will you, Sam? He can pick out the spots on a June bug in the dark."

"What is it?"

"Photos of the 'new' Sherri Starr," Ross stated flatly. "Wait till you see them. You won't believe it's the same woman."

"So you finally tracked her down." Her tone was uncharacteristically subdued. Ross had expected her to be excited by his news. Instead, she took a long, thoughtful drag on her cigarette just as the phone rang. "Yes?" she answered curtly. "No. I can't talk to him now. And hold all my calls." She replaced the receiver and picked up their conversation as if it had never been interrupted. "Have you seen her in person yet?"

"Oh, yes, I've seen her," said Ross with a wry smile. He wished he could forget how much of her he'd seen. "We just drove up to Baltimore together. She's waiting for me to pick her up at five and drive her back. I'm taking her to dinner, though she doesn't know it yet."

Both eyebrows arched this time. "I suppose you expect me to compliment you on your fast work," she said gruffly, flicking the ash off her cigarette.

Ross laughed. "I think I'd faint dead away if you did."

"I expect all it took was one look at your gorgeous puss," she said sardonically. "Hell, with her reputation, I knew she'd be easy."

"No, it wasn't like that. She's not like that at all," Ross blurted out. "Or at least she doesn't seem to be," he amended.

Sam's pale-gray eyes widened; the fascination with people that all good reporters share made them sparkle. "What's she like?"

"Not like anything you'd expect her to be from all the stories we'd heard," Ross admitted grudgingly. "She's a real classy-looking lady. She comes on soft and vulnerable and very..." He was about to say sexy but that wasn't the right word. "Sensuous." He laughed harshly. "I can see now how she managed to fool everybody and get away with murder."

"You don't know that it was murder, R.B.," Sam said sharply.

"I know it was murder," Ross returned, his tone savage. "Deliberate, cold-blooded murder."

"Are you saying that you have hard evidence?"

"No, not yet," he conceded the point, "but I will have. That or a confession." He moved close to the desk. "Buck was planning on divorcing her. He told me so himself the last time I saw him."

"Hardly grounds for murder," she returned dryly. "There'd be a lot of corpses in this country if it were."

"But, you see, he'd insisted she sign a premarital agreement before they got married." Putting his hands on the edge of the desk, he leaned toward her. "In the event of a divorce she would have ended up with a minor settlement. With Buck dead, she inherited everything."

"All right, so she had a motive," Sam said carefully, "but don't forget, the gun she shot him with was proven defective at the inquest. It could just as well have been an accident as she claims."

"Or she could have *bought* her way out of a murder indictment," Ross accused bitterly, his fingers gripping the edge of the desk so hard his knuckles turned white. "God knows, she has enough money now! Why else would she change her name and appearance? And why would she still be in hiding, three years later, if she wasn't guilty as hell?"

"That's enough, R.B.!" Sam squashed the cigarette in the ashtray and jumped to her feet. "This is not a courtroom and you are not the prosecuting attorney!"

Ross straightened up like a shot. He had to make an effort to get himself back under control.

Shaking her head, Sam walked over to one of the windows that formed the top half of the office walls, giving her a four-sided view of the copy room. "I was afraid this would happen." With an exasperated motion, she pulled the cord on the venetian blind, closing the slats. "I told you right from the start that you couldn't possibly be objective about this story. I was right."

"I like to think I'm enough of a professional," Ross returned evenly, "not to let personal feelings interfere with my work."

"I don't care how professional you are. How could they not interfere under the circumstances?" She continued walking swiftly around the room, closing the venetian blind on each window with a jerk as she passed. "Hell, Buck was

your brother. It's only natural that you'd be prejudiced
against the woman who was responsible for his death."

"I'd never allow personal feelings to prejudice my judge-
ment," Ross insisted.

"You already have," she snapped. "You said yourself
that you're convinced she's guilty of murder." She reached
for the last blind cord. "How could you possibly keep an
open mind?"

Ross knew that his editor was closing the blinds to ensure
their privacy—no one would dare enter her office when the
blinds were shut—but he had the sensation that she was
sealing off the room and suddenly felt hemmed in.

She turned to face him. "You're not after a story, R.B.
You're out to nail this woman for killing your brother."

A grim smile twisted his mouth. "I was planning to do
both."

"That settles it." With quick, resolute steps she went behind her desk and sat down. "You're off the story."

"What?"

She picked up the photo layout she'd been studying when
he first came in. "You can still do the rest of the series, but
I'm assigning the Sherri Starr story to somebody else."

"You can't do this to me, Sam," Ross said, his voice raw.

She looked up at him. The sharp lines of her face softened when she saw how upset he was. "R.B., listen to me.
I'm not talking as your editor now, but as your friend." She
replaced the layout on the desk. "I know what Buck's death
did to you. I was there. I went through it with you, remember?"

How could he forget? Sam had been the only one he could
talk to about it. His parents had never forgiven his brother
for running away from home to become a rock singer. When
Buck became famous and the stories about his escapades

and drug problems hit the papers, they were immensely relieved that he'd changed his name so no one would know he was their son. When he was killed, they claimed it was God's punishment because Buck had rejected his family's values and life-style.

Ross nodded with a heavy sigh. "I remember."

"You went after her then, after the court of inquiry had cleared her, and . . ." She paused to light another cigarette. "I never told you this before, but I was glad you were unable to track her down. I was glad to see that you'd put it behind you and were getting your life back together again." She drew in a long stream of smoke and exhaled sharply. "When I assigned this series of unsolved murders to you, it was because I knew that you were the best investigative reporter on staff. If anyone can turn up a new clue or come up with a fresh twist it's you but—"

"Sam, I—"

". . . but Buck's story," she overrode him, "was never meant to be part of the series. That was your idea. You brought that one in."

"But I didn't go looking for it, Sam," Ross protested. "I hadn't been on this assignment two weeks when my lawyer called to tell me that she was moving into the old summer place Grandma Prewitt had left Buck. Right next door to the cabin she'd left *me*, for God's sake!"

The force of his emotions propelled Ross around the desk. "Sam, she fell right into my lap . . . literally. Even the way I met her, the way she . . ." He was stopped by the memory of her clinging to him, crying in his arms, her soft breasts shuddering against his chest with every sob.

The strange look he caught on his editor's face as she stared up at him speechlessly brought Ross back to the present. "Don't you see what I'm getting at?" he insisted;

he had to make her understand. "I've never believed in destiny but it's as if it was meant that we should meet. Don't you see that?"

"All *I* see is that you're becoming obsessed with—"

"Damn it, Sam!" Ross exploded. "Wanting to bring a murderer to justice, is that being obsessed?"

"That's not what I meant," she said slowly. "It's *her* you're becoming obsessed with." She shook her head with a kind of shocked bewilderment. "If you could only see your face when you talk about her."

Ross stiffened. When he spoke, after a long moment, his voice was tight. "I don't know what you mean."

"Then it's even worse than I thought." She reached for her cigarette, which she'd left smoldering in the ashtray. "You're off the story, R.B. That's final."

"Don't do this to me, Sam."

"You're off the story!" She went back to studying the layout as if she considered the subject closed and had no intention of discussing it further.

"Sam, I owe you a lot," he got out with difficulty. "I could never forget all you've done for me. But if you take me off this story, I quit. Right here and now."

Without looking at him, she took one last, slow drag on her cigarette, then put it out. "If that's the way you want it."

"I'll get the story on my own," Ross vowed fiercely. "I've come too far to stop now. I've finally made contact with her. She's starting to trust me. She's so consumed with guilt I know it won't take me long to get the truth out of her." Bending over, he slammed his hand down on the layout, shocking her into paying attention to him again. "Sam, I can't stop until I get to the bottom of this. I've got to find out how Buck died. And I'll do it with or without your help!"

Her stunned face was a blur before his eyes as Ross wheeled around and stormed over to the door. "If you don't want the story then I'll take it to the *Baltimore Sun*." He looked at her over his shoulder as he pulled the door open. "I'm sure they'd be delighted to print it, Buck being a hometown boy and all."

"Shut that door," Sam ordered sharply, "and get back over here." She waited until Ross had come to a tense halt in front of her desk. "All right, you can stay on the Sherri Starr story."

An immense sigh of relief tore out of Ross. "Thanks, Sam."

"By the way, I don't give a hoot in hell about the *Baltimore Sun*," she added to let him know that she hadn't given in to him because of his threat. "I just want you *here* where I can keep an eye on you. Because you're heading for trouble."

"Don't worry about me." He sent her a warm, grateful smile. "You won't be sorry, Sam."

"I'm already sorry, R.B." With a heavy sigh, she reached for a cigarette—and people wondered why she smoked! "I just hope *you* won't end up being sorry."

Six

Have you been waiting long?'' Ross asked, startling Sharon.

She'd been leaning against the metal railing watching the sea gulls dip and swoop into the harbor, sunlight shimmering on their wings. She hadn't realized that he was standing a few feet away from her, and had the sudden, unnerving feeling that he'd been standing there for several minutes, studying her as intently as she'd been observing the sea gulls.

"No," she managed with a careless shrug. "Ten minutes or so."

"I'm sorry I'm late. I got tied up." His tone was casual enough but he was looking at her, his amber gaze intense and somewhat quizzical, as though he'd seen something in her he hadn't expected to.

"That's all right. I didn't mind waiting." Sharon looked out at the harbor again, at the blue-green water lapping the pilings; the soft, caressing sound the water made was as soothing as music to her. "I could look at the play of light on water for hours." She smiled wryly at herself. "I sometimes think I must have been a fish in a previous life."

Or a mermaid, Ross thought to his own amazement. The reflection from the sunlight on the water emphasized her exotic cheekbones and gave her unusually pale skin a luminous glow, making her slanting eyes sparkle. Wisps of hair clung, gleaming, to her forehead and the sides of her face and neck as if they were wet from the sea. Her lips were parted, soft and moist, and he found himself wondering whether they would taste salty if he kissed her.

With a silent curse, Ross tore his gaze away to stare, unseeing, at the glass-and-metal skyscrapers visible in the distance. Mermaid, hell, a siren was more like it. He could just see her, her wet naked body draped over a surf-flecked rock, luring unsuspecting sailors to their death with her sensuous, irresistible song.

"I'm double-parked," he suddenly remembered out loud; she'd managed to make him forget that, too.

Sharon breathed in the salty tang of the harbor, letting it out with a sigh, and pushed away from the railing with reluctant hands. "Why didn't you tell me?"

"You seemed to be enjoying the view so much," he said flatly. Without waiting for her, he started across the plaza.

"I hadn't expected to find such a quaint, peaceful spot in the middle of a big city." She was forced to hurry to keep up with his long strides. She wondered what could have accounted for the sudden change in his mood. "I didn't know Baltimore was so lovely."

He slanted her a surprised look. "Is this the first time you've been to Baltimore?" He pronounced it Bawlimawr.

"Yes. The very first time."

"Then you haven't seen the Inner Harbor yet." He put his hand lightly on her elbow as they crossed the cobblestone street that still had trolley tracks from the turn of the century winding through it.

"The Inner Harbor?" She pulled her arm away, trying not to be too obvious about it, as they stopped beside the car. She thought she caught a glimmer of amusement in his eyes; it bothered her almost as much as his touch. "What's that?"

"We'll drive by," he said as he helped her into the convertible. "It's on our way," he was quick to add before she could protest.

Sharon soon noticed that there were more spots of interest "on their way" this time than there had been when they'd driven into the city earlier. Instead of taking what had obviously been the most direct route, the Corvette now wound slowly past street after street of identical row houses with their famed white marble steps. Window screens brightly painted with landscapes added an individual touch to each home, a country charm to the city streets. Further on, waves of Victorian town houses, all intricate facades and bay windows, rode the gentle slope of the land, and church steeples pierced the sky like the masts of the famed Baltimore clipper ships that had once filled the harbor.

Riding in a convertible afforded Sharon an unlimited view and she found herself enjoying the unexpected tour too much to protest. She recalled the sign they'd passed when they'd crossed the bridge into Baltimore earlier: Welcome to Charm City. She couldn't have agreed more. She admired the diverse styles of architecture, which ranged from funky to elegant, from historical to ultramodern and the variety of ethnic neighborhoods, each with its own old-world color and heritage.

And she found herself studying her "guide" as well. Like his native city, she was beginning to realize, Ross possessed an offbeat, almost stubborn individuality. His moods were as varied and unexpected as what lay around the next corner. With his stark, uncompromising face and proud bearing, she could easily picture him astride a horse, sword at the ready, like the dashing Confederate general in the Civil War monument they'd just passed.

"And this is Mount Vernon Place," he announced, making a right turn into the nineteenth century where elegant, imposing mansions stood aloof on top of the hill like a Victorian acropolis. Mere blocks later, they were back in the twentieth century. But, as the rows of tall, concrete office buildings gave way to the glass and steel skyscrapers of Charles Center, it seemed to Sharon that they'd wandered into the twenty-first century.

Charles Center, as Ross was quick to point out, was a thirty-three acre complex, incorporating office and apartment buildings, hotels, shops, a theater, and beautifully landscaped plazas, all connected by overhead walkways that hung suspended over the traffic-filled streets. Sharon caught herself gawking like someone who'd never seen a large, metropolitan city before.

Without seeming to, Ross watched Sharon intently; curiosity, wonder, and the joy of discovery suffused her face. As he pulled into a parking space that had just opened up he wondered what her reaction would be when she saw the Inner Harbor.

She looked over at him, her eyes suddenly wary. "Why are you parking?"

"I thought you wanted to see the Inner Harbor," he said matter-of-factly.

"Yes, but I thought you were going to drive by it."

"We can't drive into the Inner Harbor," he said, as if he were surprised that she didn't know that. "This is going to have to be the walking part of the tour." Quickly, he secured the emergency brake.

Sharon frowned. As long as they were "on their way" back to St. Michaels, she hadn't minded spending the extra time with him. But to share the fun of sightseeing as though they were the best of friends was more than she'd bargained for.

"I'd really like to get home as soon as possible." Her tone made it clear that she wasn't going to allow him to presume on a friendship that didn't exist, one she had no intention of encouraging in spite of what had happened the night before.

A slow smile curved his lips. "It's the height of rush hour, Sharon, and the one and a half hour drive to St. Michaels could easily take two and a half," he told her with the conviction of experience. "Personally, I'd rather spend that hour taking in the sights than stuck in the middle of a highway. Wouldn't you?"

"Well, yes," Sharon was forced to admit, "but—"

He cut her off. "If there's one thing I hate it's driving bumper-to-bumper."

Sharon had the feeling that Ross hated constraints of any kind. Behind his carefully controlled facade she sensed a wildness that both attracted and disturbed her. Though he was leaning back in his seat, one arm resting casually on the door, he was watching her in that intent way that he had. She felt as though he were trying to read every thought in her head—as if he *could* read every thought in her head. The narrow confines of the automobile suddenly felt too close for comfort.

Sharon slid on her dark glasses. "All right," she agreed reluctantly.

With one sure, lithe motion, Ross was out of the car. Before he could get around to her side, Sharon pushed the door open and got out on her own. The wry grin that tugged at the corners of his mouth told her what he thought of her determined effort to maintain a physical and emotional distance from him.

Getting her to agree to have dinner with him wasn't going to be as easy as he'd thought, Ross realized. "The Inner Harbor is less than a block away," he informed her, keeping his tone as impersonal as a tour guide's as they started walking in that direction.

"What is that delicious smell?" Sharon inhaled deeply of the spicy aroma floating in from the harbor. "It smells just like cinnamon."

"That's what it is," Ross replied after a quick, knowledgeable sniff. "That's the McCormick Spice Co. over there. Sometimes, when the wind blows this way, the whole harbor area smells of nutmeg or paprika or black pepper... whatever they're processing that day."

"Oh." Sharon stopped in her tracks as she caught her first glimpse of Harborplace, the twin glass-enclosed pavilions reminiscent of nineteenth-century exposition halls that were the jewels in the crown of the beautifully reconstructed Inner Harbor.

Their blue-green rooftops echoed the color of the harbor waters where hundreds of pleasure boats sparkling in the sun were moored side by side on floating piers. Under colorful awnings on the ground level of the two-story-high pavilions, sidewalk cafés and restaurants teeming with people spilled out on to the wide, patterned-brick promenade edging the waterfront.

"Oh, Ross," she breathed. "This really is beautiful."

That's exactly what Ross was thinking about her. She'd removed her sunglasses to keep them from coming between her and the view, so he saw the excitement lighting up her face, glowing in the dark depths of her eyes as she looked up at him. Something tugged at his senses.

"Can we go inside?" Sharon asked enthusiastically, her cool reserve forgotten.

"Of course." He was about to take her arm but decided not to push his luck. He waved her toward the main entrance of the nearest pavilion. "Right this way."

Sharon gasped when she saw the colorful European-style marketplace of well over a hundred shops and eateries spread out before them. "You could spend the whole day in a place like this and not see everything," she told Ross with a smile.

It was the first time she'd smiled at him, a warm glowing smile, and it threw him for a moment.

"Where do we start?" The gleam of anticipation in her eyes was infectious and made Ross feel as if they were a couple of kids about to embark on a hunt for buried treasure.

It occurred to him, as they browsed through the gift shops and boutiques, that he'd never known a woman as open and spontaneous as Sharon. Her sense of adventure, her knack of finding the most unusual or drollest item, her delight in each new discovery she made were highly contagious and he found himself enjoying Harborplace in a way he never had before.

"This place is mind-boggling," Sharon said while she surveyed the stalls of exquisitely displayed candies, the mounds of chocolates and the rows of freshly baked cakes and pies.

"What can I get you?" Ross asked, amused by the child-like greed in her eyes.

"You can get me away from here." She laughed. "I must have put on five pounds just looking."

His eyes moving over her soft curves as she hurried over to the next level, Ross silently hoped that she hadn't. Her body was perfect as it was.

"And just get a whiff of *that*! The very air has to be fattening." She groaned as she took in a deep breath of the tantalizing aromas floating around them, a dizzying mixture of the varied ethnic cuisines on display. "I'm absolutely starving."

"Do you want to get something to eat?"

"Something?" She laughed again. "Everything!" The tip of her tongue, pink and wet, played with her upper lip as she scanned the assortment of Polish sausages and hot dogs, pizza and barbecued ribs, fried shrimp and steaming crab cakes. "I can't remember the last time I felt this hungry."

"Nor I," Ross murmured. But the hunger twisting inside him had nothing to do with food. It was a hunger, he had to remind himself sharply, that he had no intention of satisfying.

Impulsively, Sharon turned to Ross. "Thanks for talking me into coming here, Ross." She touched his arm, a silent apology for having resisted his suggestion before. "I would have hated to miss out on this." She felt powerful muscles tauten under her fingers as amber eyes locked with hers.

For a timeless moment they stared into each other's eyes, neither one of them able to break away. The sights and sounds of the marketplace faded. They were the only two people in that vast, teeming space, the sensual promise they saw in each other the only reality.

Then Ross pulled his arm away and looked at his watch. "It's ten to seven so—"

"Is it really that late?" Sharon broke in somewhat dazedly as she checked her own watch. She found it difficult to believe that an hour and a half had gone by so swiftly. She'd been having so much fun with Ross she'd forgotten her resolve to keep him at a distance. After what just passed between them, she wouldn't forget again.

"I have a suggestion," he said casually. "Instead of eating junk food, why don't we go out to dinner? I know a terrific little restaurant just a few blocks from here."

"No, thanks. I think we should get back to St. Michaels." Sharon slipped on her dark glasses and with them her cool reserve.

Ross stifled an impulse to pull her glasses off. He deeply resented her hiding behind them, shutting him out, but he couldn't risk antagonizing her. He hadn't given up on getting her to have dinner with him.

"I wish you'd reconsider having dinner with me," Ross said as he smoothly executed the turn onto Route 33. St. Michaels was only ten miles away and he couldn't risk taking her to dinner in town because too many people knew him. He had to make his move now.

"No, thanks." Sharon pushed her dark glasses up against the bridge of her nose. "I'm just going to grab a sandwich and get to bed early for a change."

He gave her a wry look. "I thought you were absolutely starving."

She was. It was after eight and she hadn't eaten anything since brunch. "Not really," she murmured evasively, turning away to watch the sun begin its slow descent into the bay, tingeing the sky and water a melting pink. "I think it was just being exposed to that orgy of food."

"That restaurant we're coming up on, on your right there," he persisted, slowing down so she could get a better look at it, "is one of the best seafood places on the Eastern Shore." It was now or never. He swung the car over to the side of the road.

"What are you doing?" Sharon demanded. "Can't you take no for an answer?"

"Please have dinner with me, Sharon," he asked with a self-conscious, and rather appealing, grin. "I'm not exactly looking forward to eating a TV dinner all by myself at the cabin."

That was the first time he'd mentioned the cabin all day, the first time that Sharon let herself think about the tragic circumstances of his wife's death. She warned herself against getting involved in his problems. Then she remembered what it was like to be all alone in a memory-haunted place. She looked over at him. "I've been meaning to ask you, how was your first night in the cabin?"

"Not too good. I didn't get much sleep." He neglected to add that it had been because he couldn't stop thinking about her.

"I'm sure it must have been very painful for you," she murmured.

Ross was surprised, even disturbed by the genuine concern in her voice, but he was willing to play on her sympathy if it would get her to have dinner with him. Eventually, it might even help him to trap her. "I guess that's why I'm trying to put off going back there." He forced a sigh. "I know you must think I'm a coward but—"

"Ross, don't be so hard on yourself," Sharon said, though she knew from experience that where guilt was concerned, it was easier said than done. "It's only natural that you should feel that way. You're obviously a very sensitive man."

He dropped his eyes as though he were ashamed—of admitting to being sensitive, Sharon assumed. He was a very complex man, she was beginning to realize. In an effort to reach him, she sat up and leaned toward him. "And I don't think you're a coward. I understand exactly how you feel."

"Do you?" Ross sent Sharon a hopeful smile that was not as unfelt as he would have liked. "Does that mean you'll have dinner with me?"

She sank back against the seat. Because of her dark glasses it was impossible for Ross to read the answer in her eyes. For a long, thoughtful moment she was silent. He couldn't believe that he was holding his breath.

"All right," Sharon agreed slowly, kicking herself mentally as she did. She'd spent too many dinners staring at the empty chair across the table from her, barely able to swallow her food, not to know what he was going through.

Ross shifted into drive and swung the Corvette, tires screeching, back on the road. He wasn't about to give her the chance to change her mind.

"But on one condition," Sharon added. "We go Dutch treat."

"Dutch treat?" Ross laughed out loud.

"I'm serious, Ross."

He slid her a bemused look. "Okay, if that's how you want it."

"And I also want it understood that this isn't a date." Good God, she thought, she sounded just like a teenager!

She'd expected him to laugh at her again; he nodded solemnly instead as he made a right turn into the restaurant's parking lot. "This isn't a date," he agreed, maneuvering the car smoothly into a space. "We're just two lonely people helping each other get through the night."

Helping him get through the night was not what she'd had in mind when she'd accepted his dinner invitation. His words conjured up images of her being in his bed, making love with him until he could think of nothing else, cradling him in her arms until he fell asleep. She shut out the images.

"I'd prefer to think of it as two hungry people helping each other get through dinner," she tossed back in reply.

He smiled. "Whatever you say."

Seven

The restaurant was located at the end of a converted pier that jutted out over the water. Built on thick pilings, it swayed softly with the tide. Throughout the multilevel interior, wide picture windows framed timeless seascapes and the dockside entrance where patrons moored their boats.

While they waited for the waitress to bring their drinks, Sharon studied the view. The colors of the sunset had deepened; bright slashes of orange and red tinged the sky and were reflected in the water. The reddish glow spilled through the windows, softening the edges of the rough-hewn tables and chairs and the driftwood-paneled walls. She enjoyed the illusion of being suspended in midair above the water, the sensation of the room rocking gently around her. There was something soothing, almost hypnotic, in the rhythmic sound the waves made as they lapped against the pilings.

Ross was too busy studying Sharon to notice anything else. She was still wearing her dark glasses even though they were sitting in a corner booth, out of view from the rest of the patrons, and the light from the lantern over their heads was low. The huge sunglasses hid most of her face from him but her body expressed the fascination that nature held for her.

He recalled her reaction to the harbor at Fells Point earlier when she hadn't known that he was watching her. He could still see the rapt look on her face as she'd followed the flight of the seagulls, her body straining against the railing toward the sun and the water as if she longed to be part of them. He'd never known a woman to respond so openly to each new experience. He wondered whether she gave herself that completely when she made love.

And, suddenly, he wanted to find out—if only things had been different.

"Here are your drinks," their waitress said, shattering Ross's thoughts and bringing Sharon's attention back to the table. The young girl, obviously a student, stared at the glass she was holding as if she wasn't quite sure what it contained or whom it belonged to. "Dry vermouth on the rocks?" she was finally forced to ask in a soft Southern accent.

"For the lady," Ross told her.

She flashed him a grateful smile before she set the glass before Sharon. "And a bourbon and water." Setting Ross's drink in front of him, she reached into her apron pocket for her order book. "Are you all ready to order now?"

"I haven't even looked at the menu," Sharon said, picking hers up. The hand-printed card stapled to the cover announced crab-stuffed fillet of sole as that day's special.

"There's only one thing *to* order," Ross said just as she was seriously considering the special. "You have to try the dish Baltimore is famous for."

Sharon looked over at Ross for the first time since the hostess had seated them. "What's that?"

He smiled. "Trust me on this."

Without hesitation, Sharon closed her menu and set it back on the table. "When in Rome..."

"We'll share a dozen steamed crabs," Ross ordered, "and—"

"I can't eat half a dozen crabs," Sharon protested.

"Sure you can." He sounded as though he knew her so well that he knew exactly what her capacity for food was. "And a large pitcher of draft beer."

"A *large* pitcher of—"

"Trust me," he repeated with a crooked smile. "You said you would."

Sharon threw up her hands. "All right."

"You won't be sorry," he promised as the waitress hurried off to place their order.

But Sharon was already sorry she'd agreed to have dinner with him. She wished he hadn't picked such a romantic spot—though *he* could make even a diner seem romantic. Now that they were alone again she was having trouble making conversation. Picking up the swizzle stick, she began stirring her drink.

Over the rim of his glass, Ross watched Sharon staring into the depths of her aperitif with the same total concentration with which she'd watched the sunset before. He might as well have been sitting at another table. He took a long pull on his drink. She was shutting him out again, and he resented it.

He set his glass down sharply. "You're not planning on wearing dark glasses during the entire meal, are you?"

"I'm so used to them, I don't realize I have them on half the time." She made no attempt to take them off. Instead, she took a careful sip of her drink. "Why? Do they bother you?"

"Yes," he said bluntly. "It's another one of my pet peeves, like driving during rush hour." He moved so quickly that his hand was a blur as he reached across the table and pulled off her glasses.

Sharon gasped as though he'd just removed her most intimate garment.

"I like to see a person's eyes when we're talking," he told her dryly. He held up her sunglasses. "Why do you feel you have to hide behind these?" He peered at her through the huge tortoiseshell frames. "What are you hiding from?"

"I'm not hiding from anything," she returned defensively. She moved to get back her glasses but he held them out of her reach.

He smiled wryly. "Then why do I get the feeling you're hiding a deep, dark secret?"

"Because you have an overactive imagination?" she shot back.

He twirled her glasses by the stem slowly, thoughtfully. "No, I don't think so." Probing amber eyes searched hers. "There's something behind your eyes. They look... haunted."

Sharon laughed but it came out in brittle pieces. She tried to break the connection between them and found that she couldn't. He held her with eyes that sought to see right through her, eyes the same startling shade as her dead husband's.

He leaned across the table toward her. "I told you *my* deep, dark secret last night," he said, his voice low and disturbingly intimate. "Why won't you tell me yours?"

Before Sharon could recover sufficiently to come up with a reply, the waitress reappeared at their table.

"How did your meeting go this afternoon?" Ross asked conversationally while the waitress set the large pitcher of beer and two chilled mugs at the far end of the table.

"It went very well," Sharon managed, grateful for the change of subject. She focused all her attention on her drink.

Ross folded her glasses carefully and set them next to the salt and pepper shakers. "Antiques," he said.

Startled, she looked up at him. "What?"

"I was just trying to guess what line of work you're in. From what I saw last night, I decided you must be involved in antiques."

"No." She smiled, relieved that he wasn't going to pursue their original conversation now that they were alone again. "But I have been thinking seriously about opening a shop that specializes in refurbishing antiques."

He took a sip of his drink before asking casually, "What do you do now?"

"Well, I used to be in public relations," Sharon admitted, "but—"

"Public relations?" he broke in. She wondered why he found that so surprising. "I would have thought you'd be involved in something of a more . . . artistic nature."

Now she had the feeling he was making fun of her. "No, public relations. I haven't done that since I got married and . . ." Talking about the past always made her nervous. She tucked a wayward strand of hair behind one ear. "I'm not sure I want to get into that again."

"Why not?" He seemed genuinely interested.

"You have to deal with too many people. I don't think I can take the pressure anymore. Most of my clients were in show business and..." Remembering that that was how she'd met Buck, she was unable to go on. She took what she hoped looked like a casual swallow of her aperitif. "What do *you* do for a living?"

"Me?" Ross paused to taste his bourbon and water. "What do you think I do?"

"I don't know."

"See if you can guess."

She laughed suddenly as if she enjoyed the challenge. Ross was glad to see that he'd succeeded in getting her to relax again.

She sat back against the booth and studied him for a moment. "Well, I know you're not a doctor," she murmured wryly. "You're good at fixing cars but I can tell from your hands"—surprisingly sensitive hands, she remembered— "that you're not a mechanic." Slowly, she examined the strong, uncompromising lines of his face, the fierce intelligence behind his eyes. "I'd say... a lawyer?"

"A lawyer?"

"Yes." She was sure of it now. "A criminal lawyer or...a prosecuting attorney?"

That was the second time that day someone had accused him of acting like a prosecuting attorney and it bothered him.

Sharon laughed when she saw Ross frown. "Am I right?"

"Sort of. But I'm afraid I'm just your average dull corporation lawyer."

Dull was the last thing he could be called, Sharon thought as a busboy stopped by their table.

"Your steamed crabs are comin'," the busboy announced. As Sharon watched uncomprehendingly, he spread a sheet of brown wrapping paper over the table.

"That serves as our tablecloth and dishes," Ross informed her.

"Really?" She slid the palm of her hand over the rough surface of the paper, then picked up the wooden mallet and special knife the busboy had just set down in front of her. "And what are these for?"

"The mallet is for cracking crab claws, and the knife is for digging out the meat."

She tested the weight of the mallet, and turned the knife with the short pointed blade over in her hand, delighted with the novelty of it all.

Somehow, Ross had known that Sharon would be delighted. What he hadn't anticipated was the pleasure he took in her delight. Picking up the pitcher of foamy draft beer, he started to fill their glasses. "And the beer is for—"

"I know what the beer is for," Sharon interjected dryly.

"Oh, no, you don't. You think it's just for washing down the crabs." With a playful nod he indicated the large metal tray, piled high with steaming, bright-red crabs that the waitress was carrying over to their table. "But it's really for putting out the fire. Wait till you taste the spices on those crabs."

"Here you are," the waitress said in her soft Southern drawl. "One dozen steamed hard shell crabs." Tilting the tray, she spilled the mound of crabs into the center of the table. "You enjoy 'em now."

A strong, pungent aroma drifted up with the steam from the crabs, which were encrusted with a thick layer of burnt-orange seasoning. Sharon drew in a deep breath then gasped. "What is that seasoning? It's so strong, it opened up all my sinus passages."

"It'll do that all right," Ross said with a chuckle. "That's old bay seasoning. But there's also some kosher salt, powdered mustard, and coarse-ground pepper." He shrugged out of his tweed jacket, the muscles of his shoulders and chest moving beneath his turtleneck sweater as he did. "And they're steamed in a mixture of water, beer, and vinegar." He pushed both sleeves up past his elbows, exposing lean, hard forearms and tawny hair that gleamed golden in the lamplight.

Sharon suddenly realized that she was staring. She dropped her eyes. "That sounds like quite a combination," she told the crabs.

"Aren't you going to get comfortable too?" he urged, an ironic glint in his eyes as they moved over the tailored lines of her properly buttoned suit jacket. "Once you start eating, you'll be up to your elbows in crab. The only way to enjoy them is to get down and dirty."

Trying to get out of her narrowly cut jacket while sitting in a booth was awkward and Sharon had to arch her back, causing her breasts to strain against the thin silky fabric of her blouse. Something tightened inside Ross as he recalled how her breasts had looked last night through the wet nightgown.

"They'll get you a paper bib if you don't want to risk ruining your blouse," he told her just in case she'd noticed the way he'd looked at her. It wasn't his custom to ogle a woman's body. It bothered him that he had trouble keeping his eyes off her.

"No, thanks," she said, quickly rolling up her sleeves. "Those things make me feel like a baby."

Bending forward, Ross picked up one of the crabs and held it in the palm of his hand as if he were weighing it. "Here, this one's nice and full." He set it down in front of her.

Sharon stared down at six inches of well-armored crab. "What do I do now?"

"Just follow me." Turning over the crab he'd selected for himself, Ross pried off the flap and waited for Sharon to do the same. "Okay, now, holding the crab in your left hand, put your right hand over the top of the shell, and lock your thumb under that point there."

"Here?"

Reaching over, he adjusted the position of her thumb. "That's it. Now just pull up in one even motion."

She did as she was told and the entire top shell came off in one piece. "Oh!" she shrieked, as delighted as a child. "I did it."

"That's pretty good for the first time," said Ross. "Most people break the shell in half."

Taking the shell out of her hand, he turned it over and pulled off the thick, lumpy substance in the center, discarding it. Using his knife, he scraped something out of both pointed ends and handed the shell back to her. "You can eat that."

Sharon looked down at the greenish substance swimming in a brownish liquid in the center of the shell. "You're absolutely sure about this?"

"Don't look at it, just eat it," he ordered, scraping out the points of his own shell. "It's like the tomalley in the lobster. It's one of the best parts." Tilting his head back, Ross put his shell to his lips and sucked the liquid out of it with a raw, sensual enjoyment that sent a tiny shiver up

Sharon's spine. Slowly, he licked his lips, drawing every last bit of flavor from them as he looked over at her.

When he saw that she was still hesitating, he reached across the table, and placing his hand under hers, drew the shell up to her lips. His eyes met hers over the top of the shell as she swallowed his offering. It was warm and thick, sweet and salty at the same time.

The sensually evocative moment hung between them, holding them frozen for a moment, then Ross released her hand and sat back in his seat. His touch lingering on her skin, Sharon set down the drained shell on the paper. Now she was really sorry she'd accepted his dinner invitation, but she'd certainly never expected anything like this. She should have ordered the filet of sole.

"Okay, now," said Ross, his tone that of an instructor. "Remove the lungs—those feathery things—and those lumpy pieces. Break off the claws and all the legs and save them for later." As he acted out his instructions, he watched to make sure that she was following them. "Now break it in half like this. You see all those sections inside...like a maze of almost transparent shell? There's plenty of chunks of crab meat in there but you've got to dig them out. That's where the knife comes in."

"I'd rather use my fingers," she said, attacking her food with the enthusiasm and sense of adventure he'd seen in her earlier. He thought of what it would be like to have her turn that sense of enthusiasm on him.

"These are really delicious," Sharon mumbled around a moist, briny morsel. "I've never tasted crabs quite like these. They're as sweet as lobster but much saltier. They taste of the sea."

Ross took a long, lusty swallow of beer. "You've never had blue fin crabs before?"

"No." Her tongue flicked out to catch a stray bit of crab meat clinging to her top lip and draw it into her mouth. Ross found himself wishing he were a crab. "Only Dungeness crab."

"That's right," he murmured, forcing himself to concentrate on his food. "You're from California."

Sharon froze. How did he know where she was from? Did he also know her real identity or was that what he was trying to uncover?

Carefully, she studied the lean, uncompromising lines of his face, the single-minded concentration with which he pursued his task. For the first time she noticed the way he was using his knife to pick the crab clean. The sharp, pointed blade was like an extension of his hand, probing every corner, cutting through the brittle inner walls, exposing layer after layer. There was something scary about such thoroughness. The pale skeletal shell was all that was left when he was through.

"How did you know I was from California?" Sharon asked, trying to keep her voice steady.

Ross picked up instantly on the tension underlying her tone. He would have mentally cursed himself for his thoughtless slipup if his mind hadn't already been racing to find a logical explanation. He finished cracking open a crab claw with his hands before looking up at her. She was watching him warily. He gave her what he hoped was his most disarming smile. "You've got California license plates on your car."

A sigh of relief escaped Sharon and she was able to breathe again. "I've been so involved with fixing up the house, I haven't had time to change them." She smiled wryly. "For a moment I thought you were a mind reader."

First Class Romance

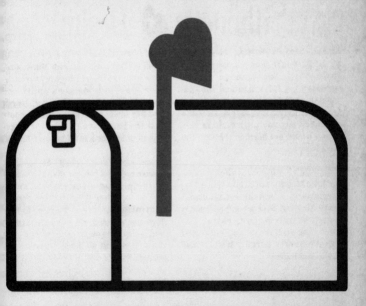

Delivered to your door by

Silhouette 🖤 Desire®

(See inside for special FREE books and gifts offer)

Find romance at your door with 4 FREE NOVELS from...

Silhouette ❤ Desire®

Elaine Camp's HOOK, LINE AND SINKER. Roxie was a reporter for *Sportspeople*. Sonny Austin was the country's top fisherman and the subject of Roxie's next interview. It wasn't long after they'd met that Roxie knew she would pay any price to make sure Sonny would not become the one that got away.

Joan Hohl's A MUCH NEEDED HOLIDAY. For Kate Warren, Christmas was a time of emptiness—until she met handsome Trace Sinclair. And what had been a contest of wills began to change into something else, something only their hungry hearts dared admit...and would not let rest.

Diana Palmer's LOVE BY PROXY. Amelia Glenn walked into Worth Carson's board room wearing only a trenchcoat and a belly dancer's outfit, she was determined to do her act. Worth had her fired, but Amelia didn't know that the handsome tycoon was determined to bid for her on his own terms!

Laurel Evans' MOONLIGHT SERENADE. Emma enjoyed life in the slow lane, running a radio station in a small town. So, when TV producer Simon Eliot invited her to give a speech in New York she refused. So, why did Simon keep returning on weekends? And why did Emma wait so desperately for his arrivals?

OPEN YOUR MAILBOX to these exciting, love-filled, full-length novels. They are yours *absolutely FREE along with your Folding Umbrella and Mystery Gift.*

AT-HOME DELIVERY. After you receive your 4 FREE books, we'll send you 6 more Silhouette Desire novels each and every month to examine FREE for fifteen days. If you decide to keep them, pay just $11.70 (a $13.50 value)—with no additional charges for home delivery. If not completely satisfied, just drop us a note and we'll cancel your subscription, no questions asked. **EXTRA BONUS:** You'll also receive the Silhouette Books Newsletter FREE with every book shipment. Every issue is filled with interviews, news about upcoming books, recipes from your favorite authors, and more.

Take this FOLDING **UMBRELLA** *and a Mystery Gift as an* **EXTRA BONUS!**

CLIP AND MAIL THIS POSTPAID CARD TODAY!

Silhouette ❤ Desire®

SILHOUETTE BOOKS, 120 Brighton Road, P.O. Box 5084, Clifton, NJ 07015-9956

☐ **YES!** **Please send me 4 FREE NOVELS** *Plus my* **FREE UMBRELLA** *AND* **Bonus Mystery Gift**

I understand that you will send me my four Silhouette Desire novels along with my FREE Folding Umbrella and Mystery Gift, as explained in the attached insert. I am under no obligation to purchase any books.

Name	(please print)

Address

City

State   Zip

Terms and prices subject to change.
Your enrollment subject to acceptance by Silhouette Books.

Silhouette Desire is a registered trademark.   CMD 106

Take this beautiful
FOLDING UMBRELLA
with your 4 FREE BOOKS
PLUS A MYSTERY GIFT

CLIP AND MAIL THIS POSTPAID CARD TODAY!

NO POSTAGE
NECESSARY
IF MAILED
IN THE
UNITED STATES

BUSINESS REPLY MAIL
FIRST CLASS   PERMIT NO. 194   CLIFTON, N.J.

Postage will be paid by addressee

SILHOUETTE BOOKS
120 Brighton Road
P.O. Box 5084
Clifton, NJ 07015-9956

"Hardly," muttered Ross. He wished he were. But he was beginning to see how her mind worked. Being distrustful wasn't part of her nature, it was something she'd learned recently.

"I'm sure they don't prepare crabs this way in California," he went on in an attempt to keep the conversation going and get Sharon to relax and open up again. "This is strictly a Maryland specialty." Tossing the empty claw on to the pile of shells littering the paper, he reached for another crab. Seeing that Sharon had finished hers, also, he picked one out for her as well. He was surprised to find that she'd kept up with him, not an easy achievement for a beginner. "I'm delighted to see you like steamed crabs. I had a feeling you would."

"How could anyone *not* like them?" With one sure motion, she pulled off the top of the shell. "They're so delicious."

"True, but some people don't like to go to so much trouble to eat them."

She laughed. "But that's part of the fun." With spice-coated fingers she removed and discarded the inedible parts exactly as he'd shown her.

She was a very bright, aware person, Ross warned himself, and he'd better not underestimate her again.

"Is it my imagination," Sharon asked between bites, "or are the crabs getting spicier?"

"I think the spices just start getting to you after a while," Ross replied with a crooked smile. "Especially when you've got them all over your fingers as you do."

"I enjoy eating with my fingers," she said, enthusiasm lighting up her slanting brown eyes. "That's part of the fun, too."

"As long as you enjoy your meal."

"This isn't a meal," she returned after taking a long swallow of frosty beer, the perfect accompaniment to the hot, spicy crabs, "it's an experience."

All of her senses felt heightened somehow. The skin on her fingertips tingled from the spicy, gritty seasoning; tiny moist bits of crab meat clung to them and to her lips. Her tongue and the roof of her mouth burned from the hot spices and were soothed by the cold foamy beer. She could hear the waves crashing against the pilings, feel the room moving gently around them as if they'd been set adrift and were floating out to sea. The salty tang of the sea mingled with the intoxicating aroma of the spices swirling around them.

And she was aware of Ross as she'd never been aware of a man before. The amber glow of the lantern swinging overhead highlighted the rugged lines of his face, making his eyes gleam a pale gold. At his every movement, the lean, hard muscles of his shoulders and arms rippled with an easy masculine grace that barely hinted at their power. As if mesmerized, she watched the way his lips closed over every juicy morsel.

His slow, thorough manner of eating was deceptively detached looking, she realized. He actually experienced as much enjoyment from his food as possible, prolonging the sensual pleasure it gave him almost indefinitely. Yet she also sensed a need in him to control his appetites as if they were much stronger than he would have liked. She wondered what would happen if he ever really let go.

A wry smile curved his lips as though he'd read her thoughts. Only then did Sharon realize that she'd been staring at him, a crab claw in one hand, the wooden mallet poised in midair. He leaned across the table toward her. "Something wrong?"

"No...uhh, yes," she stammered, pointing with the mallet. "I was just noticing that you've got a tiny piece of crab meat at the corner of your mouth."

His tongue flicked out lazily to catch it. "And *you* have one on your chin." Ross would have loved to lick it off, to lick her lips clean of the fragments of crab clinging to them. Impulsively, he reached across the table and, before she could get to it, lifted off the piece of crab. Slowly, deliberately, he put it into his mouth and ate it.

The blatant sensuality of his gesture, the even more disturbing intimacy of it threw Sharon totally. Her mouth went dry. Rattled, she hit the crab claw hard with the wooden mallet, pulverizing it.

Ross laughed. "Don't worry, it's not going to bite you." Shifting the knife to his left hand, he picked up his mallet. "Here, let me show you a better way."

Placing the edge of the knife just below the toothed part of the claw, he hit it once with the mallet, merely cracking the top part of the shell. Picking the claw up in both hands, he twisted it, snapping the rest of the shell easily. His fingers were so strong and supple it didn't surprise Sharon that anything would give way to them. He slid the meaty part out of the shell in one long piece. Leaning across the table, he offered it to her.

Without thinking, Sharon opened her mouth. His eyes locked with hers just as her mouth closed over the claw, encompassing the entire length of it. Heat flowed under her skin, and she was sure that her face was as red as any of the crabs. She pulled back, but that served only to pull the succulent meat off the claw. There was nothing to do but to eat it.

A surge of hunger went through Ross that had nothing to do with food. Her action had been completely spontaneous, all the more sensuous for not having been calculated. From the blush suffusing her face, he could almost believe that she didn't know just how sensuous a woman she was. He'd never felt more confused in his life.

He tore off the top of the shell and lifted it to his lips to block out the sight of her face, all flushed. But he drank the juices out of it as hungrily, as thoroughly as he secretly wanted to drink the moist warmth of her mouth.

Still feeling embarrassed, Sharon buried herself in the mercifully intricate business of eating the crabs. So did Ross. Neither of them spoke for several long minutes.

It seemed to Sharon that their every movement—the way she sucked the crab meat from her fingertips, the way his teeth bit into the moist white meat before drawing it into his mouth—had suddenly become suggestive. The simple acts of chewing and swallowing were taking on disturbingly sexual connotations.

"I used to think crabs were ugly, even a bit scary-looking," she said in an attempt to fill the unnerving silence hanging between them. "But now I realize how beautiful they really are."

With a critical eye, Ross examined the hard, spiky shell of the crab he'd just opened. "You call this beautiful?"

"Yes," she replied without looking up from her food. "I think a crab's shell is one of nature's most unique achievements."

Ross suppressed an ironic smile. He could see why she would relate to a crab's shell. If she could, he was sure, she would crawl inside one and hide forever.

"Nothing can penetrate it," Sharon continued between bites. "And in its natural color, it provides perfect camouflage."

"Nothing provides perfect camouflage," Ross told her. "There's always someone who can see right through the disguise."

Sensing a double meaning in his words, a touch of sarcasm, Sharon looked up at him.

"And there's always someone out there who's specially equipped to penetrate even the hardest shell," he added, dismantling the crab with one easy motion. He grinned disarmingly. "That's a law of nature."

"Yes, I...I suppose it is," Sharon murmured. For an instant she'd felt a sense of danger. She'd thought he had that look of a predator she'd glimpsed in him last night in the moonlight. She told herself she was imagining things again. "Well, at least they don't feel anything," she insisted, going back to her food. "They're so well protected by their shell, nothing can get in to hurt them."

"There's only one thing wrong with living in a shell." He cast a glance at her dark glasses, making it clear that he wasn't referring to the crabs. "Nothing can get in, but nothing can get out either." A wry smile tugged at his lips when he looked back up at her. "Besides, even crabs have been known to shed their shells when properly motivated."

"Really?" Reaching for her beer, Sharon sent him a wry smile of her own. "And what do they consider proper motivation?"

"Making love," he drawled while with expert fingers he continued working the meat out of a crab leg. "Just about the best motivation there is." His eyes met and held hers. Slowly, he sucked the meat out of the shell.

Her mouth burning from the spices, Sharon took a long swig of beer. As she licked off the foam clinging to her top lip she caught Ross staring at her mouth. His lips parted in unconscious response.

"You know," he murmured, never taking his eyes off her mouth, "in spite of their hard shells, crabs happen to be very tender lovers."

Sharon was so startled by his comment that she laughed. "Crabs are tender lovers?"

"By fish standards they are," he replied seriously before attacking another leg. "Most male fish are wham-bam-thank-you-ma'am kind of lovers. All they're interested in is mating with a female and then leaving her to fend for herself." He shook his head proudly. "But not your Maryland blue fin crab."

"You're putting me on."

"No, I'm not." Ross paused to crack a claw with his fingers. From the corner of his eye he could see the high, round curve of Sharon's breast straining through her silk blouse. He lifted the claw and slowly drew the moist pink meat out ot the shell with his teeth. He took his time devouring it. "You see, in order to make love, a female crab has to shed her shell, which leaves her totally defenseless—"

"Well, I'm glad I'm not a crab," Sharon interjected sardonically.

He laughed, a deep, sexy rumble of a laugh that went right through her. "It's not as bad as you think." He leaned across the table toward her. "Just before she sheds her shell, the male wraps his whole body around hers"—with spice-coated fingers and surprising sensitivity he recreated the movement of one body wrapping itself around another—"and he holds her that way until she's ready."

Sharon forgot to chew. Without realizing it, she leaned across the table toward him.

"Even after they've made love he doesn't let go of her," he went on, his voice soft and deep, his warm breath brushing her face. "He clings to her," his hands tightened into possessive fists, sending a shiver through her, "covering her naked body with his own. And they move through the water that way, for miles sometimes, for as long as it takes for her new shell to harden."

Sharon swallowed quickly. "Really?"

Ross nodded. "Now that's what I call tender loving." His tone had a wry edge to it but the look in his eyes as they searched hers was disturbingly intense. "Wouldn't you?"

"Yes," Sharon breathed. Remembering how Buck used to roll over and go to sleep after making love without so much as a word, she couldn't help feeling that man could learn a lesson or two from the crab. She wondered what kind of lover Ross would be.

His eyes narrowed as though he'd read the question in hers. The warm, sexy smile he gave her sought to answer it. Sharon sat up in her chair.

"There's only one thing I don't understand," she said coolly, a bit defensively. "Why is it, when it comes to love, that it's always the female who has to shed her defenses? Why can't the male shed his defenses too?"

"Because he's the one who has to protect her," Ross returned without hesitation.

Sharon laughed. Ross had never known a laugh could be so full of pain.

"But who will protect her from him?"

Eight

Sharon's question haunted Ross throughout the rest of the meal. As he maneuvered the car into her driveway, he turned the question over in his mind one more time. What could have happened to make her so bitter about men? he wondered. He slid her a look as if he might find the answer on her face.

Eyes closed, she was resting her head on the leather-upholstered headrest. He could tell from her breathing that she wasn't asleep, but she hadn't said a word during the short drive back to St. Michaels. At least she wasn't wearing her dark glasses again. Her short hair was windblown from driving in the open convertible, her skin soft and luminous in the moonlight. There were no traces of hardness or bitterness in the exquisite lines of her face, just an indefinable sadness.

Had Buck been the one who'd hurt her so deeply that she was now afraid to trust another man? Was that why she'd struck back at him? Maybe greed hadn't been her motive for killing him, after all.

Because of the nature of his job, Ross had always prided himself on being able to size up people quickly and accurately. It hadn't taken him long to realize that she wasn't the calculating, mercenary woman he'd initially thought. Nor was she capable of playing games like most women he knew. But she was extremely emotional and impulsive. Could it have been a crime of passion instead of cold-blooded murder?

He had to remind himself that it didn't make any difference.

Through the thick fringe of her lashes, Sharon glanced furtively at Ross. What could he be thinking of so deeply? she asked herself. The intensity of his presence reached out to her no matter how much she tried to elude him. Even with her eyes closed, the awareness of the long, hard body sitting close to hers had tugged at her senses. She couldn't understand why this man should have such an effect on her. She felt as nervous as a schoolgirl on her first date, frightened and strangely happy at the same time.

"We're here," Ross announced, turning off the motor.

Sharon's heart skipped a beat. What on earth was the matter with her? They weren't on a date and she certainly wasn't an inexperienced schoolgirl. She sat up.

He turned around in his seat to face her. "Are you okay?"

"Yes, fine."

"Could I interest you in an after-dinner drink?" he asked, one hand resting casually on the steering wheel.

"No, thanks."

"It's still pretty early," he insisted, his tone soft, almost pleading.

Sharon was sure that Ross was trying to put off being alone in the cabin. She felt for him, but she didn't know if she could handle being alone in such an intimate setting with him. She'd never gotten so close to someone so quickly and it confused her. "Do you have a TV?"

"What?"

"Because if you don't," she went on, "I have a small portable one I can lend you."

A bemused smile played on his lips. "What for?"

"In case you have trouble sleeping again," she explained. "It really does help."

Ross could think of something that would help even more. But the way he felt about her at that moment—her eyes warm with concern, her lips parted, soft and vulnerable—he had to revise his thought. If he had her in his bed neither one of them would sleep all night.

His fingers tightened around the steering wheel as he reminded himself who she was. The hunger she'd aroused in him at dinner, which he thought he'd conquered, was back, clawing at his insides. "No, thanks," he replied evenly. "I have a TV."

"Well, let me know if you need anything," Sharon offered, trying not to notice how the moonlight made his eyes gleam pure gold, how surprisingly sensitive his mouth was. "Good night then. And thanks for dinner."

"I'm the one who should thank you. It's been a very long time since I've enjoyed a day this much." He was somewhat amazed to find that he really meant it.

"I enjoyed it too." Sharon couldn't remember when she'd enjoyed a day more. It bothered her that she was sorry to see it end.

"We'll have to do it again then," he said, his voice soft and deep, full of promise.

Sharon meant to tell him that that was out of the question, but she couldn't. Nervously, she brushed her bangs out of her eyes, and caught a whiff of the tangy aroma that clung to her hand. "That's strange."

"What?" He watched as she sniffed the tips of her fingers.

"I scrubbed my hands with soap and water and they still smell of crabs." Bringing both hands to her face, she inhaled deeply. "My hands smell just like the sea." She laughed, a bubbly, childlike laugh of delight that was absolutely irresistible. "Here, smell." Eyes sparkling, she held her hand impulsively up to his face.

Before he could stop himself, Ross grabbed her hand and buried his face in it. Avidly, he drank in the salty tang that clung to it and tasted the warm, moist sweetness of her flesh.

Sharon gasped when she felt his lips trailing hungry little kisses over the sensitive skin of her palm but she was too stunned to do anything. With his tongue, he traced the length of her fingers, slowly, erotically, one by one. When his teeth closed over the fleshy part of her palm, sending something like an electric shock through her, she pulled her hand away.

"No!" he grated as though she were denying food to a starving man. His hand shot out and, gripping her wrist in midair, pulled her over to him.

Her cry of surprise was lost in the groan that tore out of him when his mouth took hers. Taut arms locked around her, crushing her to him until she could barely breathe. His mouth moved on hers with a burning hunger, igniting a passionate longing in her such as she'd never known, shattering any thought of resistance. She suddenly realized how

much she'd wanted him to kiss her. The hands she'd pressed
to his shoulders to push him away clung instead.

He moaned on her mouth when he felt her respond to
him. As if he'd been starving for the taste of her, he kissed
her over and over again, deep devouring kisses that were almost frightening in their intensity. Only when they were
both gasping for breath did he finally drag his mouth away.

"I've been dying to do that all day," he got out raggedly.
"That, and more." His eyes darkened as they searched her
face. He smiled when he saw that she was too dazed with
passion to do anything to stop him. "This..." Bending his
head, he nibbled the corner of her mouth with barely controlled hunger, making her gasp. "And this..." With his
teeth, he tugged on her bottom lip, drawing it into his mouth
where he sucked on it. "Especially this." He thrust his
tongue deep into her mouth as if he meant to fill her up with
him, long, hard thrusts that left her shaking uncontrollably.

A rush of tenderness went through Ross when he felt her
breasts shudder against his chest. She seemed overwhelmed
by sensations she'd never known and could barely handle.
Her delicate arms went up to grip his neck as if she were
drowning and he was the only one who could save her. His
kiss gentled without losing any of its intensity. He could feel
her mouth heating under his as she opened up to him. He'd
never known a woman to give herself to him like that. Suddenly, he wanted to make her feel how much he wanted her,
to feel her all over him.

"This car wasn't built for this sort of thing," he muttered thickly, impatiently. Sliding his right hand from
around her back, he reached blindly under his seat for the
lever he knew was there. One tug and the seat slid back sev-

eral inches. Grabbing her by the waist, he lifted her the rest of the way out of her seat and onto his lap.

The abrupt movement almost brought Sharon back to her senses but his fingers sank into the rounded curves of her bottom, pulling her up against him. An uncontrollable shiver went through her when she felt him, hot and hard, through the layers of their clothing. Swiftly, his hands moved, pushing her open jacket out of the way to capture her breasts.

Sharon's breath caught in her throat when his questing thumb found a budding nipple; when his mouth closed over it avidly, her breath escaped in a ragged rush. The flimsy fabrics of her blouse and bra proved no barrier to the moist heat of his mouth or the hungry tug of his teeth. Her whole body contracted against him.

Eager for the feel of her skin under his hands, the taste of her in his mouth, Ross began to undo the buttons on her blouse. When she felt the cool air on her heated flesh, Sharon pulled away abruptly, her back slamming into the steering wheel. The piercing scream of the horn shattered the silence of the night, shocking them both back to reality.

Sharon was dazed, unable fully to comprehend what had just happened. Ross seemed even more amazed than she. He didn't make a move when she slid clumsily off his lap back onto the other seat, or even when she pushed the door open and stumbled out of the car. Her legs were shaking so much she could barely stand. She fell back against the door, shutting it behind her. Overwhelmed by a barrage of conflicting emotions—shame, excitement, guilt—she had to grip the top edge of the door to steady herself.

With a curse, Ross dropped his head back against the headrest. He couldn't believe he'd let himself lose control—with her of all people! He waited for his heart to resume beating normally, for the throbbing heaviness in his loins to dissipate. He had to make a conscious effort to think clearly. He was sure he'd wrecked the budding friendship he'd nurtured so carefully between them, which was essential to his plan to trap her.

Raking an angry hand through his hair, he looked over at her. She was still leaning against the car door with her back to him. In the bright moonlight he could see that she was shaking. It took him a moment to realize that it was because she was crying.

He sat up. "Sharon, are you all right?" When she didn't answer, he jumped out of the car and went over to her. "I didn't hurt you, did I?"

She shook her head without looking at him.

"I'm sorry, I...I didn't mean to be so rough," he said in a low voice. He'd never grabbed or kissed a woman like that in his life, nor had he ever wanted to, and he certainly hadn't intended to make love to her. He sighed heavily, disgusted with himself for having been unable to resist her. "I really didn't mean that to happen," he added, his voice grim. "I'm sorry."

"You don't understand," she said miserably, looking up at him. "I wanted it to happen." Fresh tears filled her large slanting eyes and spilled down her face. "I wanted you to make love to me."

For a moment, Ross was too thrown by her honesty to react. Would she ever cease to amaze him? "Then why are you crying?"

"I don't know, I—I guess it's because..." Another wave of guilt swept over her, making it difficult for her to go on, but she felt she owed him an explanation. "Because you're the first man I've...been with since my husband died."

If she'd told him that yesterday, Ross would have laughed in her face. He wasn't laughing now.

"I never thought I could feel this way again...that I could want someone even more than—" Shocked by her own words, Sharon stopped herself. She laughed brokenly, even a little hysterically as she brushed away the last of the tears. "This whole thing is crazy. I don't even know you. We've barely met."

"That's the way it happens sometimes," said Ross tightly. Until that moment he would never have believed it could happen that way either. Why did it have to be with her?

"No!" She shook her head wildly. "No, it doesn't happen that way," she insisted, trying not to notice how the lingering flush of passion softened the rugged lines of his face; his mouth was still wet from hers.

A wry smile twisted his mouth and his eyes glided slowly down to her body.

Following the line of his gaze, Sharon saw that the top buttons on her blouse were still undone, exposing her lacy bra and the high slopes of her breasts. She reexperienced the thrill that had gone through her when she'd felt the warmth of his hands on her breasts, the hungry tug of his mouth.

"The only reason it happened," she resumed, determined to find a logical explanation for her behavior, "is because we...we sympathize so much with each other." With trembling fingers, she started fumbling with the blouse buttons. "We've both lost someone we loved under tragic circumstances and...and tonight we were lonelier than usual so—"

Ross cut her off with a sardonic laugh. "You don't really believe that, do you?"

She looked up at him, her eyes wide, tears glistening on her lashes. Her bottom lip trembled as she tried to say something but couldn't.

Ross had to stifle the urge to grab her and pull her into his arms, to kiss her until she shook uncontrollably again to prove to her that all her arguments were sheer nonsense. No one wanted to believe them more than he did. He shoved both hands deep in his pants pockets before he did something he knew he would regret.

"I don't know *what* to think anymore," Sharon murmured. With a hopeless gesture, her hands fell to her sides. All the buttons on her blouse were secured again but she could still feel the patch of silk where his mouth had left a warm wet circle clinging to the tip of her breast. "But I do know one thing." Turning around abruptly, she reached into the convertible for her pocketbook. "We can't see each other anymore."

Slinging the pocketbook over her shoulder, Sharon started resolutely toward the street entrance to her house.

Ross came after her. "Why not?"

"Because I have certain...problems I still have to work out, Ross. Until I'm free of the past, I can't even think about getting involved with someone." She looked at him pointedly as she rounded the corner of the house. "And with your problem, neither should you."

"We're already involved," he said grimly.

"No, we're not! We just got carried away for some reason but—"

"Sharon, listen to me," he cut her off, his voice thick with emotion. "I never meant that to happen. It won't happen again, I promise." It was a promise Ross also made to himself—and to his brother's memory. "You're right about one thing, neither one of us is ready to handle a romantic involvement right now, but there's no reason why we can't still be friends."

She stopped in front of the door and looked over at him, surprise mingling with wariness in her eyes.

"I meant what I said before," Ross persisted, stepping in front of her. "I can't remember the last time I enjoyed being with someone so much...that I enjoyed just being alive and having a good time." He didn't have to fake the emotion in his voice, he was telling the truth. "I think we could help each other. There were times today when I completely forgot about the past. You did, too. I know you did."

With a reluctant nod, Sharon tugged her keys out of her purse.

Ross continued to stand directly in front of the door, making it impossible for her to open it. "I can help you to finally break free of the past, Sharon."

"I wish it were that easy," she murmured ruefully.

"You'll never be free of the past as long as you keep running away from it," he told her, his voice deep and warm, strangely seductive. "One of these days, you're going to have to face what happened. I'd like to be there when you do."

Taking the key from her hand, he unlocked the door for her then stepped to one side. "Let's just take it one day at a time," he pleaded with a soft smile as he handed her the key. "All right?"

Sharon's hand was shaking when she accepted the key from Ross. She hesitated as she was about to step inside. "All right," she agreed, her voice barely audible. She was shaking deep inside when she closed the door behind her.

A sigh of relief that was half a curse escaped Ross. He should have been glad that his argument had won Sharon

over but he wasn't. He knew the reason he'd pleaded with
her so convincingly had nothing to do with Buck; it was because he didn't want to stop seeing her.

As he turned to walk the short distance to the cabin, he
recalled what Sam, his editor, had accused him of earlier.
She was right, he *was* becoming obsessed with Sharon. Yet
he felt all the more compelled to find the proof that would
convict her—if only to stop himself from falling in love with
the woman who had killed his brother.

"Aha, caught you lying down on the job," Sharon called
out playfully to Ross as she crossed the lawn carrying a
pitcher of iced tea in one hand and two frosted glasses in the
other.

"*Sitting* down on the job," he corrected her without
looking up from the sports section of the *Examiner*; the rest
of the Sunday papers were strewn over the picnic table.
"Besides, until you decide what you want to keep and what
you want to throw out—" he nodded in the direction of the
motley assortment of items in the driveway that they'd spent
the better part of that morning clearing out of the garage"—there's nothing more I can do."

Sharon thought she detected a note of irritation in Ross's
tone. He'd started the day in a cheerful mood, but as the job
of clearing out the garage progressed he'd become more and
more uncommunicative. She wondered whether he was
sorry that he'd offered to help her now or whether he was
just in one of his moods.

He was usually very easy to be with. They'd been spending a lot of time together since their dinner almost a week
ago, canoeing and crabbing and taking long leisurely strolls
through the countryside. As he opened up to her more and
more, she was surprised to find that he was capable of great

warmth and sensitivity and had a rather droll sense of humor. But often, sometimes when they were having the most fun—usually when they were having the most fun—he would suddenly grow quiet and moody, withdrawing to someplace deep inside him, somewhere unreachable.

Sharon was sure that Ross's unresolved guilt about his wife's death was responsible for his dark moods. She'd been experiencing guilt feelings of her own because of her undeniable attraction to Ross. As he'd promised, he hadn't made a move toward her since that night, but there was always an undercurrent of sexual tension between them. Sharon realized that she was falling in love with Ross, and there were times when she felt that he was beginning to care about her too. She was starting to believe that happiness was possible for her again—for both of them.

Her eyes moved over him like a caress when she stopped in front of the picnic table. Like her, he was wearing an old work shirt and jeans; they clung to the long hard lines of his body as she wished she could. She had to stifle an urge to brush back the lock of tawny hair that had fallen onto his forehead, to smooth away the tension tightening the rugged lines of his face.

"Is everything all right, Ross?" she asked softly as she began filling the glasses.

Ross was surprised that Sharon had picked up on his mood; he'd always prided himself on being in control of his emotions. "Sure." He shrugged nonchalantly without looking up from the paper. He certainly couldn't tell her that rummaging through Buck's old possessions had stirred up forgotten boyhood memories and a gnawing sense of guilt. He felt like a traitor. And it was all because of her.

Every day when he got up, he swore to himself that he was going to finally spring the trap on her. The more he got to know her and realize how sensitive and emotional she was, the more he knew his trap would work, finally forcing her to reveal the truth about Buck's death. Every night before he went to sleep, he told himself that he was right to have put it off, that it wasn't necessary to make her confess because she was starting to trust him. But in trying to get her to open up to him, he was opening himself up to her in a way he never had with any other woman. Most of the time when he was with her now, he didn't even think about Buck.

It was time to spring the trap.

"I really appreciate your helping me clean out the garage," Sharon said, setting the pitcher on the table. She gave him a warm smile. Her sun-dappled skin glowed with the golden tan she'd acquired over the last week, and that haunted look was gone from her eyes. She'd never looked lovelier—or more desirable.

Ross warned himself not to get caught in *her* trap. With an irritable rustling of paper, he turned to the next page. "I was just wondering what you were planning to do with all that stuff."

"There are a few things I'd like to keep," she replied, sliding onto the long bench across the table from him. "Whatever I can't use, I'll give to the Salvation Army."

"There are a couple of things I might be able to use," Ross stated matter-of-factly. "I'll pay you whatever you think they're worth."

"You don't have to pay me," Sharon said. "Take anything you want."

"I'd like that bicycle." He indicated the ten-speed bike, now dented and paint-chipped, that had been one of Buck's most cherished possessions as a teenager. "And that stringless guitar over there." Something wrenched inside Ross whenever he looked at his brother's first guitar.

"I have a nephew," he went on in response to the surprised look she was giving him, "who would get a big kick out of them."

"That's great." She took a long swallow of iced tea.

"You sure you don't mind parting with that guitar?" he asked, watching her carefully.

Sharon looked away. The last thing she needed was another painful reminder of the past. "I have no use for it."

Buck's childhood mementos obviously had no meaning for her, Ross thought angrily. He was glad she was making it easy for him to do what he had to do. He forced a smile. "Would you like to see the paper?"

"No, thanks. I stopped reading newspapers. They're too depressing." There was an uncharacteristic note of resentment in her voice. "All they ever write about are crimes and wars and people getting killed."

"Well, if you don't care for the news—" Ross picked up the magazine section "—how about the *Sunday Magazine*?" He handed it to her with a casual gesture. Without seeming to, he waited for her reaction to the cover.

The cover was a collage of news photos from the thirties—a close-up of a revolver, the dead body of a man lying in a pool of blood, a theatrical photograph of a voluptuous, dark-haired woman—spread out on the background of a blowup of an enormous estate. Her eyes widened as she scanned the headline: NEW EVIDENCE LINKS TORCH SINGER LIBBY HOLMAN TO UNSOLVED KILLING OF MILLIONAIRE HUSBAND. AN IN-DEPTH REPORT BY R.B. HUNTLEY.

She shook her head disapprovingly. "You see, that's just what I mean."

"It happens to be a very interesting article," said Ross, trying to encourage her to read it. He couldn't wait to see her reaction.

She opened the magazine and flipped slowly through it to the article, as if she was reluctant to read it yet felt compelled to in spite of herself. Over the top of his paper, Ross watched the growing tension on her face as she read it.

When she turned to read the last page, Sharon's attention was caught by the announcement that was printed in a box at the bottom. She felt a sudden, painful constriction in her throat as she read: "This is the first in a series of weekly reports examining, among others, the unsolved killings of television star Bob Crane and rock idol Buck Starr." The magazine slid out of her hands onto the table.

"Did you finish the article already?" Ross asked, trying to keep his tone conversational.

"No, and I'm not going to!" Sharon was unable to contain the anger that was twisting her stomach into knots. She couldn't believe that the press was going to drag up the story of Buck's death again. Her name and face would be plastered all over the papers once more, the most intimate details of their life together, distorted beyond recognition, would be spelled out for everyone to gloat over. Would there never be an end to it? She slammed the magazine shut.

Ross had known that Sharon would identify with the Libby Holman case but he hadn't expected her reaction to be so strong. To him it was a clear indication of her guilt. "What's the matter, Sharon?"

"I just think it's terrible the way this..." She stared at the byline as if she meant to memorize the name. "This R.B. Huntley is trying to pin a murder on a woman who can no longer defend herself."

"I didn't think he was trying to—"

"A murder she probably didn't commit," Sharon cut him off. "My God, the woman's been dead for years and they still won't leave her alone! Why are people like that?"

"There's something about an unsolved murder that affects people on a very elemental level," said Ross dogmatically. "I think it has to do with the sense of outrage we all feel when someone kills another human being and gets away with it.

"Besides," he went on quickly before she could protest, "there's always something fascinating about a mystery. Especially one with so many unanswered questions." His eyes locked with hers. "For instance, what could have happened between husband and wife that night to drive her to shoot him? Was it jealousy? Revenge?" He searched her eyes as though he might find the answer there. "Or did she do it for the money?"

"How do you know she did it at all?" Sharon returned defensively. "They never found any evidence that she murdered him."

Ross smiled coldly. "She could have destroyed the evidence."

"But it was well known that her husband was an emotionally unstable man. It might have been suicide or an...an accident."

"No, it wasn't an accident," he said, his voice sure and hard. "Or suicide."

"But that was the coroner's verdict," Sharon protested as though they were arguing her own innocence or guilt instead of Libby Holman's. "That's why the case never went to trial."

"She could have bribed the coroner." His eyes slid down her body. "Or she might have used her considerable charms to sway him."

"You want to believe she's guilty!" Sharon cried. "Why does everyone always want to believe the worst about people?"

"I don't *want* to believe she's guilty," Ross countered, suddenly on the defensive himself. "I'm not expressing an emotional opinion. I'm only interested in the facts."

"The facts," Sharon repeated sarcastically. "As if mere facts could ever explain the reasons people do the things they do."

"If you find the facts, you find the reasons. And the fact is she had both motive and opportunity."

"What motive?"

"If you had finished reading the article, you would have found that out."

"I don't have to finish the article to know what it says," Sharon shot back contemptuously. "I know how easy it is for reporters to distort the facts to fit their preconceived theories. All they care about is coming up with an angle that's guaranteed to sell more papers."

Ross had never done that in his life and he was stung by her accusation. "If you're not going to discuss this logically," he bit out, "then there's no point in discussing it at all!"

Sharon smiled wryly. "Now who's being emotional?" She was glad that she'd succeeded in getting a rise out of him. She resented his cool, know-it-all attitude about something he couldn't possibly know anything about. "All right, since you're the one who's in charge of the fact and logic department, what *was* her motive?"

"Her husband had found out that she was having an affair with his best friend. Their house guests heard them quarrelling about it."

Sharon shrugged off his explanation. "The lover could have killed her husband. He was also one of the guests."

"But he didn't have anything to gain by killing him since the husband was already set on divorcing her. She was the one who had everything to lose."

She laughed, a short, bitter laugh. "It's always the woman who has everything to lose, isn't it?"

He leaned across the table toward her, fixing her with a hard stare. "If her husband had divorced her as he'd threatened, she wouldn't have gotten a cent of his fortune." A harsh smile twisted his mouth. "It isn't easy for a woman to give up a life of luxury once she's grown used to it."

"Are you speaking from experience or is that a fact?" Sharon responded coldly. "You don't have a very high opinion of women, do you?"

"Not of some women, no."

She laughed. "I wonder if you realize how self-righteous you sound. It must be wonderful to be so idealistic, to expect—no, demand—perfection from people. Haven't you ever done something you're deeply ashamed of?" Her eyes had that haunted look again as they searched his deeply. "Something you may not have meant to do but . . . that you can't forgive yourself for?"

"No," said Ross, his voice hard. "Never."

"That makes you a very rare person indeed, Ross." She smiled ruefully. "It also explains why you can be so intolerant of other people's mistakes."

"We're not talking about mistakes!" Ross snapped. She'd just shown him a side of himself he'd been unaware of and it bothered him. "We're talking about a woman who killed her husband and didn't pay for her crime!"

"But she did pay for it," Sharon cried, "even though she was innocent!" In some strange way, Sharon believed that if she could convince Ross of Libby Holman's innocence she could get him to believe in her own when she eventually told him who she was.

"What happened that night destroyed the rest of her life," she went on, shaking with emotion. "For the rest of her life, everywhere she went she was pointed out as that woman who killed her husband and got away with it. All of her friends, even her own family could never be sure of her innocence. Whenever people looked at her, she could see the question in their eyes, that refusal to believe anything but the worst."

The strange look on Ross's face brought Sharon to a halt. She was sure he must be wondering why she was acting as if she were being personally accused of the crime.

"Anyway, the point I was trying to make," she continued, trying to give him a logical reason for her outburst, "is that the way she was hounded by the press, who kept digging up the story every time there was a shortage of axe murderers, it's no wonder she eventually took her own life."

He fixed her with a long, cold stare that sent a shiver of fear through her. "Maybe it was because she couldn't go on living with the guilty secret she kept locked inside her."

For an instant, Sharon felt that Ross *was* talking about her, that she'd given herself away somehow. But even if she hadn't, she knew now that she could never tell Ross the truth about herself. He would never forgive her for having lied to him. Happiness wasn't possible for them, after all. With a sinking feeling, she wondered whether he would recognize her when Buck's story was rehashed in the papers. She couldn't bear to see that look she'd been running away from in *his* eyes.

Her hands were like ice as she pulled herself up from the table. "I think I'd better start sorting out those things," she told him. "Was there anything else you wanted besides the bicycle and the guitar?"

"No, that's it," he said, getting to his feet as well.

In silence they walked across the grass to the driveway. Out of the corner of his eye, Ross studied Sharon. Her every move telegraphed a kind of despair; she looked like a condemned woman going to the gallows. She would never be more vulnerable than she was at that moment, he realized.

Now was the time to spring the trap.

Nine

I've been meaning to give *you* something," Ross said as he pushed the door to his cabin open. He walked the bicycle inside and propped it up against one wall.

"Really?" Clutching the stringless guitar, Sharon hesitated in the doorway. She'd never been inside Ross's cabin before. "What?"

"Just something I think you should have."

"What could...oh, Ross," Sharon exclaimed as she caught her first glimpse of the interior. "This is beautiful!"

"It could use a bit of straightening up," said Ross, hurrying over to his desk. Quickly, he pulled the cover down over his portable typewriter and gathered the pages of the article he'd written. He dropped the pages on top of the folder filled with clippings and news photos relating to Buck's death. Wondering whether she'd noticed anything, he glanced over his shoulder. She was too busy taking in the decor.

"But everything's as neat as a pin," Sharon continued as she admired the rustic decor of the log cabin.

Because of its soaring height, the single room gave the impression of spaciousness while the ingenious use of levels and partitions created several smaller, cozy rooms that afforded a feeling of intimacy. The tan leather couch and matching armchairs grouped invitingly around the large stone fireplace formed the living room. Two rows of free-standing bookcases set at an angle created the study; the dining area could be glimpsed through the spaces in a partition made of slats. A rough-hewn wooden staircase built into one wall led to the sleeping loft that hung below the wooden rafters.

The dark, rough-hewn wood that was also used for the walls and the floor made the sunlit view from the high windows seem even brighter. Gleaming white shafts of light streamed into the room through the branches of the pine trees encircling the cabin, creating the illusion of being deep in the forest. It was hard to imagine that a murder had been committed in such an idyllic setting.

There wasn't a single feminine touch anywhere, Sharon suddenly realized. Had he deliberately removed any touches his wife had added to the decor or had it always been that way? The cabin was as blatantly masculine as its owner, the lines of the colonial furniture as lean and stark as the lines of his face and hard, rangy body. Splashes of red in the boldly patterned throw rugs and wall hangings and the huge quilted bedspread added vibrant color to the room, hinting at the innate sensuality of its owner.

Sharon's eyes glowed when she turned to Ross. "This is really beautiful, Ross."

Ross was surprised to see that Sharon was enchanted with his summer home. He would have thought it not glamorous enough for her. "I'm glad you like it," he murmured, pleased. He sent her a warm smile, which she returned, and the chill that had been between them, a last remnant of their argument, dissolved.

Ross had to remind himself why he'd brought her there. The sight of Buck's guitar dangling from her hand helped him harden himself against her. "Come on in," he invited while he pulled the rolltop down over his desk, hiding everything from view.

Reluctant to intrude on his memories, Sharon continued to hesitate in the doorway. But there was more to it than that, the sudden quivering in the pit of her stomach told her. They had not been alone indoors since the first night they'd met. The very intimacy of the secluded cabin added to the nervous excitement that was causing her pulse to speed up. "I really think I should finish sorting things out."

"This won't take long," he assured her as he made his way over to her. "Here, let me have the guitar." Taking Buck's guitar from her, Ross hung it by its strap from the clothes tree next to the door. Putting his hand lightly on her back, he drew her inside, closing the door behind them.

"What is it you wanted to show me?" She was so aware of his touch that it took an effort to keep her tone casual.

"Not show you, *give* you," said Ross as he led her over to the study. The warmth of his hand penetrated her light cotton blouse, lingering on her skin when he released her to get something out of the locked drawer of his desk. "Here it is." A wry smile twisted his mouth. "No home should be without one."

Sharon stared down at the bundle wrapped in a man's linen handkerchief that Ross had just placed in her hand.

The object wasn't much longer than her hand but had a solid weight to it. "What is it?" she asked, smiling in anticipation.

The smile froze on her face when she unwrapped the corners of the handkerchief to reveal a hand gun—the exact make and model of the revolver that had misfired, killing her husband. A strangled cry tore out of her as she thrust the revolver back into his hands, the handkerchief fluttering to the floor. "I don't want that."

"You shouldn't be alone in the house without any protection," he insisted. "If I'd bought this gun two years ago, my wife might still be alive."

"I don't believe in having guns around the house," Sharon got out the words with difficulty. She could barely breathe from the painful constriction in her chest. "Anything . . . can happen."

Ross had lain awake nights wondering what Sharon's reaction would be when she was confronted with the weapon she'd used to kill Buck. Guilt was written all over her face. He moved in on her. "But this is the perfect weapon for a woman," he assured her; he might have been a salesman demonstrating a product. "It's light and easy to handle." Holding the gun out in front of him, he took aim at a bookcase. Her eyes widened and the blood drained from her face. "Yet powerful enough to inflict considerable damage."

"I know," she said, her voice barely audible. "That's why I don't want it."

"Just try it," Ross persisted, grabbing her wrist with his free hand to keep her from walking away as she'd intended. "Here, just get the feel of it."

Sharon tried to twist free of his grasp but he was too strong for her. She gasped when she felt the cold hard metal against the skin of her palm, the deadly weight. "No!" She pulled her hand away violently, sending the revolver crashing to the floor. The sound of metal slamming against wood was lost in the explosion of a gunshot. Sharon screamed and staggered back.

Ross was too stunned to move. He'd never seen such naked terror on a person's face.

"Oh, my God, Ross," she cried brokenly, "you're not..."

"No, I'm all right," he muttered distractedly. How could she be concerned about him after what he'd just done to her?

"Thank God, I—I thought I'd..." Bursting into tears, Sharon threw herself into his arms. "If anything had happened to you..." Desperately, she clung to him, burying her face in his chest to block out the images flooding her mind.

There was so much blood... and she could do nothing to stop it!

"I told him I didn't want the gun," she stammered between deep convulsive sobs. "He insisted I take it...he made me take it. He made me—"

"Who, Sharon?" Sliding his hand in her hair, he drew her head back so he could see her eyes. "Who are you talking about?"

"My husband. I—I killed him!" Another paroxysm of sobs convulsed her and she buried her face against his chest again.

Ross could feel her delicate body shaking uncontrollably against his. He was sure that if he hadn't been holding her up she would have collapsed. He certainly hadn't expected anything like that. "Come and sit down," he murmured in her hair. Wrapping his arm around her, he led her over to the couch. "Now tell me what happened."

She drew in a long breath then let it out in broken shreds. "I could see that he was high on cocaine," she murmured, staring ahead of her as if she were seeing what she was talking about. "His eyes had that unnaturally bright look to them and... and he was moving about in that quick, nervous way, raving on and on about plots against his life and... and how he was going to be assassinated just like John Lennon because—"

"Why should anyone want to assassinate him?" Ross broke in incredulously.

"That had become an obsession with him." Wiping away the tears with trembling hands, Sharon looked over at Ross. "My husband was a famous rock singer. Do you know who Buck Starr was?"

"Yes," Ross said, his voice flat. "I know who he was."

"Then you must also know how he died, how I..." Tears flooded her eyes again and she was unable to continue.

"All I know is what I read in the papers." Now, more than ever, Ross had to know the truth, yet he hesitated; he didn't want to hear her admit her guilt. But he'd come too far to turn back now. "What really happened, Sharon?"

Sharon felt herself caught and held by the emotional intensity of Ross's gaze but in *his* eyes there was none of the ghoulish curiosity that she was used to seeing. He leaned toward her until his face was barely inches away from hers. "Tell me about it," he urged softly.

"We'd had a terrible fight that afternoon," she found herself admitting. "I didn't want him to go on the road because I knew he was strung out on coke again. I begged him to cancel the tour and go back to the sanitarium for treatment but—"

"He'd been in a sanitarium?" Ross couldn't help cutting in; that was something his brother hadn't told him.

"Yes. He'd been hooked on drugs for years before I met him." A rueful smile flickered over her tear-stained face. "Behind that brash, cocky facade Buck showed the world was a lost little boy who wanted desperately to be loved."

That was the most insightful description of Buck he'd ever heard, Ross had to admit. He'd thought *he* was the only one who'd known that about his brother.

"I think the reason he married someone like me," she went on, "was because he knew that, unlike the leeches he'd surrounded himself with, I really cared about him. But I agreed to marry him only if he went to a sanitarium for help...and he did."

She brushed the bangs out of her eyes, which suddenly glowed with pride. "He stayed off drugs the whole first year of our marriage. It was the happiest year we ever had. But, then..." The light went out of her eyes. "Then he began slipping back again and there was nothing I could do about it."

"Why? What happened?"

"He didn't have a single hit record that year, and his concerts weren't selling out as they used to. His manager blamed me...and finally, so did Buck." Sharon shifted around on the couch to face Ross. "I kept telling him his music was good enough to stand on its own," she insisted defensively, still trying to win an argument that was long lost. "And that he didn't need the kind of audience who came just to see him smash guitars to pieces or...or any of the other crazy stunts he'd pull when he was stoned. But he wouldn't listen to me." A defeated sigh escaped her. "He accused me of deliberately trying to ruin his career."

That was exactly what Buck had told him about Sharon the last time they'd met. "But why would he accuse you of ruining his career if you were really trying to help him?"

"Because he was suffering from paranoid delusions brought on by his cocaine addiction. You wouldn't believe some of the stories he used to tell about me when he was like that."

"Like how you'd gone to bed with every member of his band at one time or another?"

Sharon let out a tiny gasp of surprise. "How did you know about that?"

That was something else Buck had told him at their last meeting. "I must have read about it in the papers," Ross murmured evasively.

"The papers!" She laughed bitterly. "They never chose to print *my* explanation of that story. It didn't make for as exciting copy." With dark, intense eyes she looked up at him, her lashes glistening with tears. "There was never any truth to that story, Ross," she told him as if his believing that meant a great deal to her.

"I know there wasn't," Ross returned sincerely. The luminous smile she gave him tugged at something inside him. He had to remind himself that although her reasons had been emotional rather than mercenary, she had still murdered his brother. "Why did he give you the gun, Sharon?" he asked bluntly.

The anguishing memory of that night brought Sharon to her feet. "He'd started stashing guns all over...in the house...the car. He even carried one on him all the time." Without realizing it, she began pacing in front of the couch. "He was obsessed with the idea that someone planned to break into the house while he was gone so he insisted on showing me how to use a gun in case they did. It was a revolver, just like...that one." She halted and turned slowly to look over at the gun that was still lying on the floor in the middle of the study. "*Exactly* like that one."

Sharon's eyes darkened as she continued to stare at the revolver. Ross held his breath while he wondered whether she was questioning such a remarkable coincidence. Though she tried, Sharon couldn't drag her attention away from the gun or stop the flow of memories it evoked.

"He said shooting a gun was the easiest thing in the world," she murmured as if she were in a trance. "I told him I didn't want the gun but he made me take it. He placed his hand over mine... his hand was like ice." A shiver went through her. "And then he put his index finger over mine on the trigger. I remember how I jumped when he pulled the trigger. He laughed at me because he'd told me the safety catch was on. He showed me how to aim again, then insisted I try it on my own."

She paused to swallow convulsively. "I pointed the gun into the fireplace." Ross watched intently as Sharon raised her arm, pointing with her thumb and index finger like a kid playing cops and robbers. "Not even bothering to take aim, just wanting to get it over with. 'No, that's not right,' Buck yelled and he stepped in front of me just as I pulled the trigger." Her arm fell slowly to her side. "I remember thinking how light the tension on the trigger was when I heard the shot."

She seemed totally unaware of the tears that were streaming down her face again. "Buck just stood there for a moment, very still, this strange look of surprise on his face and then he... he crumbled up before me." Sinking slowly to her knees, she stared down at the rug as if she could see a terrible vision within its bright-red pattern. "I don't remember dropping the gun or running over to him, just kneeling down beside him and... and all the blood gushing out." She wrapped both arms tightly around her middle, trying to choke off the sobs threatening to convulse her again. "I felt so helpless. I didn't know what to do. There was nothing I could do, nothing! Except watch him die."

Covering her face with both hands, Sharon gave in to the sobs racking her body; there was no other sound in the room. Ross had neither moved nor spoken during her entire confession. When she looked up at him a sob broke off in her throat and the tears froze inside her. He was staring at her, an indecipherable look on his face. He seemed unable to move, to even begin to deal with what she'd just told him. He was the only person she'd ever trusted enough to tell about Buck's death, except for the police or those involved in the inquest. If he didn't believe her...

"Police ballistics proved that the safety catch on the gun was defective," Sharon insisted desperately. "That's why I was never indicted, not even on a manslaughter charge. But, somehow, everybody else refused to believe it was an accident." A chill spread through her. "Ross, *you* believe me...don't you?"

"Yes," Ross said roughly, blinking back the tears that were stinging his eyes. He jumped to his feet and went over to her. Bending down, he pulled her up off her knees. "Yes, I believe you."

"Oh, Ross, you don't know how much that means to me." Her misty eyes sparkled with joy, making her face radiant, blinding him. "I was so afraid that if you knew the truth about me, you wouldn't like me anymore."

"Like you?" he repeated brokenly. He took her face in his hands; with strong, warm thumbs he wiped away her tears. "I *love* you, Sharon." Bending his head, he dragged kisses over her wet eyelids, all over her face, until his mouth found and caught hers.

She threw her arms around his neck, giving herself up to him without hesitation. Never had he known a woman to give herself to him so completely. He wondered how he could have ever believed she was capable of harming anyone. Her lips softened, opening under his at the first searching thrust of his tongue. He moaned when he tasted the moist sweetness of her mingling with the salty tang of her tears. A rush of tenderness such as he'd never known for any other woman went through him.

A sigh of regret escaped Sharon when Ross lifted his mouth from hers. Her eyes fluttered open and she looked up at him wordlessly, dazed by the intensity of the emotions and sensations spiraling through her. His hands slid up to tangle in her hair.

"Do you love *me*?" he demanded fiercely.

"I know I haven't known you long but..." With trembling fingers, she reached up to trace the rugged lines of his face as if she couldn't quite believe this was actually happening. She laughed softly, a bit incredulously. "Yes, I do."

"I've wanted you from the first moment I saw you," Ross finally admitted to himself as well. "I've never wanted a woman so much." A strange smile twisted his lips. "If you only knew how hard I tried to keep from falling in love with you."

"Because of your wife?"

Ross knew that he should tell Sharon the truth now, before things went any further, but he hesitated. He was afraid the love he saw glowing in her eyes would turn to anger—or hatred. This wasn't the right moment to tell her, he rationalized; he'd hurt her enough for one day.

Sharon saw Ross's hesitation, the look of guilt darkening his eyes at the mere mention of his dead wife.

"Let's not talk about the past anymore," he bit out. "Let's not even think about it." His hands moved to grip her arms almost painfully. "There's just *now*, just you and me." He pulled her up against him, his face blocking out everything as his mouth came down on hers.

Sharon was stunned by the intensity of Ross's kiss; there was a kind of desperation in it, and an almost frightening hunger. He wrapped his arms around her as if he meant to surround her with himself, to wipe everything out of her consciousness except the burning crush of his mouth, the tightly coiled feel of his body. Mindlessly, she surrendered herself to him.

Ross groaned with joy and relief when he felt Sharon's body melt against his. Longing to fill her up with him, he thrust his tongue deep into her mouth. He ached to bury himself inside her, to lose himself in her, making love to her until nothing existed for her except him.

"Just you and me," he repeated when he lifted his mouth mere inches from hers so that they were still sharing the same breath. "That's all that matters now." He searched her eyes intensely. "Isn't it, Sharon?"

"Yes!"

As if all he'd been waiting for was her approval, his hands began to move over her body while his mouth took hers again in a kiss that shivered all through her. Gliding over her breasts, his fingers found the buttons on her shirt and undid them quickly. In his impatience to hold her naked in his arms, he threw the shirt aside.

Swiftly, he found and unhooked the front closing on her bra. Going down on his knees before her, he covered the slopes of her breasts with hungry kisses, his fingers slipping between the bra and her skin to peel off the lacy scrap. "You're so beautiful," he murmured, his hands swallowing up her breasts possessively. "So beautiful it almost hurts."

His teeth caught the budding tip of her breast, making her gasp; with barely controlled hunger he drew it into the moist heat of his mouth. Her whole body contracted against him and she had to grab his shoulders to steady herself. He made a sound at the back of his throat when he felt her nipple harden with excitement against his tongue but never stopped swirling warm, wet caresses over her.

He continued even when his hand released her breast to tear open the snap and zipper on her jeans, sliding inside to touch her. Sharon caught her breath at the double assault on her senses. Her nails bit into his shoulders as she felt the tug of his lips and teeth on her breast, the burning touch of his hand seeking and releasing the liquid heat of her.

Feeling her response to his touch excited Ross almost beyond control. More roughly than he'd intended, he tugged off her jeans and panties in one motion, pulling her sandals off with them.

Her face flushed, her breath coming in gasps, Sharon watched dazedly while he ripped off his own clothes. "Oh, Ross," she breathed, her eyes moving over the lean, hard lines of his body with a kind of wonder. "*You're* the one who's beautiful." With trembling hands, she reached out to caress him when he stepped back over to her but she never got the chance. Aching for the feel of her, Ross hauled her into his arms once more.

"Kiss me," he ordered fiercely, eager hands moving over her in an effort to fit her soft contours to his long, hard frame.

"Yes!" But without her high-heeled sandals, Sharon's head barely reached the middle of his chest. She had to go up on her toes to meet his waiting lips.

He laughed softly, his heated breath brushing her up-turned face. "You're so tiny."

"Not everyone has long legs," she reminded him wryly.

"I think I can take care of that problem easily enough." The same seductive promise gleamed in his golden eyes as his hands moved to clutch her rounded bottom, lifting her effortlessly several inches off the floor. Sharon moaned as he slid her body up his, flesh caressing flesh, until their torsos met at every point.

"Hang on tight," he ordered. "I'm taking you to bed."

"Like this, up those stairs?"

"That's right."

She laughed huskily, making his blood jump. Love and desire glowed in the dark depths of her eyes as she threw her arms unhesitatingly around his neck and wrapped her legs tightly around his hips. A rush of heat shot through Ross. He couldn't wait. Digging his fingers into the rounded flesh of her bottom, he lifted her over him; with one thrust he was deep inside her.

A shudder went through both of them at the impact and they shared the same cry. Sharon's body arched like a cat's as she felt herself touched more deeply than she'd ever been touched before. Ross had to force himself to be perfectly still: she was on fire, all liquid fire surrounding him, and he knew that if he moved inside her, just once, he would lose all control.

He slid one arm under her and the other around her shoulders, holding her securely against him. "Where's that kiss you promised me?" he whispered raggedly as his mouth reached hungrily for hers. Mouths melting together, arms wrapped tightly around each other, bodies joined in the most intimate of embraces, he carried her up the stairs to the bed loft.

The back wall of the loft was of glass, suspended like a tree house among the green, sun-dappled pines surround-

ing the cabin. Sharon was amazed that it was still day outside, that there was still a world out there. Brilliant shafts of
sunlight streamed through the tall trees into the loft.
Branches swaying in the breeze formed shifting patterns of
light and shadow over Sharon's naked body when Ross
lowered her onto the bed, slipping out of her embrace.

She gasped when she felt the cool air on her flesh, the
emptiness inside her. "Ross?" She raised her arms to him
in a gesture that mingled love and need.

"I don't want it to end just yet," he explained. "Do you
mind?" He didn't wait for her answer. She couldn't have
answered him if she'd tried. Sitting on the end of the bed,
he bent over and ran both hands slowly, searchingly, over
the high curve of her insteps, up her silky calves and thighs.
With long, sensuous strokes he worked his way down again.
His hands closed around her ankles, parting her legs, and he
slipped between them.

Trailing heat, his hands continued moving up her body,
lingering over the swell of her hips and belly, the soft undercurve of her breasts. His gaze was another kind of caress, just as heated and as shameless as the pleasure he found
in her body. Sharon wasn't used to being looked at or
touched with such disturbing intimacy. She felt totally exposed.

"Ross, please," she begged, her legs shifting restlessly
against him. Lifting her arms, she sought to pull him down
on top of her. "Please..."

"Not yet." His hands shot out to grip her wrists. Spreading her arms out wide, he pinned them softly, but firmly, to
the bed. "Not until I've touched and tasted every inch of
you." Powerful thighs shifted to trap her ankles beneath
them, making it impossible for her to move. A tiny shiver of

fear went through her when she realized how vulnerable she was.

Slowly, thoroughly, his mouth began retracing the path his hands had taken. Her breath caught in her throat when he covered her swollen breasts with feverish kisses and bites; it rushed out of her with a moan when he slid his tongue down her body.

Ross was stunned by the hunger ripping through him. The hunger he'd known with other women had always been easily satisfied. But with her it gnawed at all his senses. He couldn't get enough of the feel of her skin under his hands, the intoxicating smell and taste of her. The helpless little cries she uttered, the tremors that shook her delicate body at his every touch intensified his excitement, making him want to prolong her pleasure indefinitely.

A sudden longing to know the taste and texture of her desire took hold of him, a longing to make her his in a way he never had any other woman. When he heard her shocked intake of breath as his mouth claimed her intimately, he knew it was a new experience for her, too. A rush of love and tenderness such as he'd never been capable of before went through him, melting into his blood. With burning little kisses he opened her up to him. His mouth adored her.

Overwhelmed by sensations she'd never known, had never even dreamed existed, Sharon twisted beneath him, trying to break free, if only for a moment, so that she could catch her breath and her heart stopped pounding so violently. But the way Ross had her pinned to the bed, she was unable to move, to do anything to dissipate the intensity of the pleasure coiling almost unbearably inside her. Only when he felt her shuddering on the edge of ecstasy did he release her. With one powerful movement, he rushed up her body and buried himself deep inside her.

His name was a strangled cry on her lips when she felt the full extent of his possession and she held on to him with every part of her. Waves of liquid fire and engulfing heat washed over her, threatening to consume her. With each powerful thrust of his body, she felt herself coming apart bit by bit. Soon there would be nothing left of her. A shiver of fear gripped her at the unaccustomed sensation, stalling the urgent rhythm of their movements.

"Don't hold back on me," he pleaded fiercely. His arms tightened around her and his body crushed hers deep into the mattress as if he meant to surround her with himself. "I want you to give me all of you." He dragged kisses on her burning eyelids and trembling mouth while his body urged hers on with deeply possessive thrusts. "I won't let go until you give me all of you!"

His fiercely loving vow snapped what little resistance was left in her. She felt as if the outer layer of her skin were a protective shell that was now cracking, disintegrating, exposing the soft, vulnerable flesh inside. She couldn't tell where she ended and he began anymore. As one, their bodies convulsed, shuddering violently. As one, they were swept away in a mindless, blinding ecstasy. Lost to their own selves, they finally found their true selves in one another.

Ten

What number Lancaster Street?" Ross asked, slowing down as he drove past the colorful rows of remodeled Federal buildings.

"It's that light-blue building over there," Sharon replied, pointing.

As he pulled into a parking space, Ross wondered whether Sharon would allow him to go in with her. She hadn't kept the location of the building a secret, as she had when he'd driven her to Fells Point two weeks before, but she hadn't told him what her appointment was about either.

"How's that for door-to-door service?" he asked when he helped her out of the car.

"Not bad," she teased. "I think I'll hire you."

A little perplexed, he smiled as he read the bronze plaque over the main entrance. "School of the Performing Arts? Are you planning on taking up an instrument?"

"No, of course not," she murmured evasively. "Look, this won't take long, Ross. Five, ten minutes at the most."

"Do you mind if I come in with you rather than wait in the car?"

Surprised by his request, Sharon hesitated a moment. Now that Ross knew her real identity, there was no reason why he shouldn't come in with her. "If you like."

"Singing lessons?" he persisted with a teasing smile while he held the door open for her. "Is that what you're signing up for?"

She laughed. "If you'd ever heard me sing, you wouldn't ask that question."

"What then?"

She hesitated again as she made a sharp right down a hall she'd obviously been down before. "I've arranged with the school to set up a music competition to award cash prizes and scholarships in Buck's name," she finally admitted, looking somewhat embarrassed. "I thought it would be a good way to use the royalties that are still coming in from his music and records."

"That's quite a remarkable thing to do, Sharon."

"Not really." She gave him a rueful look. "I just wanted to do something to keep Buck's name alive."

Neither one of them spoke again until they came to a halt in front of a large oak desk. "I'm Mrs. Farrell," Sharon told the handsome woman behind the desk. "Mr. Morgan is expecting me."

A smile of recognition lit up the older woman's face. "Yes, of course, Mrs. Farrell. You're to go right in." Her elegant bone structure, the graceful way she got up and all but floated over to the paneled door proclaimed her an ex-ballerina. She knocked twice on the door before opening it to announce, "Mrs. Farrell is here, Mr. Morgan."

"Ah, Mrs. Farrell." The dapper, white-haired gentleman rose to his feet. "Do come in," he urged, hurrying over to them while his secretary closed the door silently behind her.

Sharon quickly made the introductions and while the two men shook hands, she unzipped the inside compartment of her attaché.

"Won't you sit down?" Mr. Morgan offered, indicating the section of his office where four plush armchairs circled a cocktail table. "May I get you something? Coffee, a drink perhaps?"

"No, thanks," Sharon replied, handing him the envelope she'd removed from her case. "I just stopped by to drop off the check for the prize money."

"Ah, wonderful," the director exclaimed when he'd slid the check for fifty thousand dollars out of the envelope. "This will be a great help to our students financially, and an inspiration as well. They all know and admire Buck's music. Why, he's become our most famous pupil."

"He often spoke of the time he spent here as the happiest in his life," Sharon admitted.

He gave Sharon a grateful smile. "But I wonder if I might ask another favor? We would be most honored if Mrs. Starr would present the awards to the winners."

"No, that's not possible," Sharon said, a shade too forcefully. "Mrs. Starr is still in seclusion."

"The competition is a memorial to her husband, after all," the director continued. "Don't you think she would want to be there to honor him personally?" He turned to Ross as if seeking his support.

"Yes, I agree," said Ross without hesitation.

Sharon's eyes widened with surprise. "It's just not possible," she told Ross, her tone making it clear that she wanted him to mind his own business.

"Maybe if *I* spoke to her," Mr. Morgan persisted. "I might be able to impress on her the importance of her presence at the first competition. With her there, we would get full press coverage and—"

"Mrs. Starr hates publicity of any kind," Sharon cut him off, her voice shaky. "Mr. Morgan, we agreed that this was to be a completely anonymous donation. But if you're not going to keep to your agreement, then—"

"No, no, no," the director hastened to assure her. "I wouldn't think of going back on our agreement." He looked at Ross, clearly hoping to find an ally; when Ross said nothing, a resigned sigh escaped him. "Very well. But I would greatly appreciate it if you would inform Mrs. Starr of my request."

"It's no—" Sharon started.

"We'll give it a try," Ross finished for her. "The least we can do is ask her," he added before Sharon could protest. He gave her a wry smile. "You never know, she just might change her mind."

"Splendid. Splendid." Luckily the director was too overjoyed to catch Sharon's annoyed look. "That's all I ask." With a new excitement in his step, he preceded them to the door. "The competition will be held four weeks from this Saturday," he cheerfully informed his new ally, giving up on getting any assistance from Sharon. "I'm confident that once you've explained the symbolic importance of Mrs. Starr's presence, she will agree to attend."

"We'll get back to you on that," Ross assured him. Sharon was simply too flabbergasted to speak. Before she could recover, Ross grabbed her arm and propelled her ahead of him out the door.

She waited until they were out on the street again before turning to him. "Ross, why did you do that?"

"Because I think it's time you stopped running away from the past and faced who you are, Sharon."

"Please, let's not start in on the past again," she implored as they walked over to the Corvette. "It's too beautiful a day, and you promised to show me the sights and take me to dinner, remember?"

"Okay," he relented with a smile, but his eyes were deadly serious. "But we have to talk about this later."

"Later," she agreed, grateful for even the smallest reprieve.

Ross was aware of the irony in his trying to get Sharon to admit her real identity while *he* was still pretending to be someone else with her. Only his fear of losing her had kept him silent that long. But he'd reached the point where he couldn't keep silent any longer and go on living with himself.

As he slid behind the wheel of the car, he resolved to tell her the truth when they got back to the cabin later that evening. It wasn't going to be easy; he wasn't sure how she would take it. He had to find a way to make her understand why he'd had to lie to her so she wouldn't end up despising him...but how?

That question nagged at him for the rest of the afternoon and all through dinner. During the drive back to St. Michaels he suddenly hit on the answer—it was the perfect solution to both their problems.

While he lay in bed waiting for Sharon to finish undressing and join him, Ross carefully weighed the words in his mind one more time, trying to strike a balance between truth and justification. He felt as if he were composing the most important story of his life.

As she tossed her blouse onto the chair already littered with his clothes, Sharon shot Ross a worried look. Undressing had always been a mutual experience with them, all searching caresses and impatient little kisses. But tonight he'd quickly undressed himself, and now he was just lying there staring up at the beamed ceiling, oblivious of her presence.

Had she said or done something to upset him? Or were memories from the past tormenting him again? She paused as she was about to unhook her bra. "Is everything all right, Ross?"

All the carefully chosen words flew out of Ross's head when he looked over at Sharon. She was standing next to the bed in her bra and panties, her skin glowing soft and lustrous in the light from the bed lamp. The glow of love that was lighting up her eyes came from within. A sudden fear seized him. He tried shrugging it off. "Sure. Everything's fine."

"Then what were you thinking of so seriously?"

His eyes held hers for an endless moment; when he finally spoke, his voice was low, barely audible. "I was thinking how much you mean to me."

She laughed wryly as she slipped out of her bra. "You didn't look too happy about it."

The bra went flying out of her hands as he grabbed her impulsively by the waist, pulling her down onto the bed. "Because I don't know what I would do if you stopped loving me," he grated, burying his face between her breasts.

"Oh, Ross." Tears misted Sharon's eyes as she slid her hands into the tawny tangle of his hair, drawing his face up to hers. "Don't you know how much I love you?" Placing soft kisses on his eyelids, she traced every rugged line of his face with her lips until they found his.

Ross moaned when he felt her mouth open to him. He slid his tongue deep inside, eager for the warm honey taste he could never get enough of. Her arms went up to twine around his neck and her body surged passionately against him. The feel of her skin on his, the soft crush of her breasts sent the blood pounding through his veins. It would have been so easy to make love to her, to tell her the truth about himself afterward while her body was still drugged, her mind still dazed from their lovemaking—easy and unfair.

He pulled away. "No. We've got to talk."

"Talk?" She laughed breathlessly. "Now?"

"Yes." He reached up to pull her arms reluctantly from around his neck, then rolled over to the other side of the bed. He needed to keep his distance from her in order to think clearly. "It's important."

Sharon was about to protest but saw the determination in his eyes. She slipped under the covers, pulling them up to her shoulders, suddenly feeling cold. "What is it?"

"I think you should accept Mr. Morgan's offer to give out the prizes at the competition."

"No." She shook her head forcefully. "No, I can't do that."

"How much longer are you going to go on hiding from the rest of the world, Sharon? And just what are you hiding from? Don't you realize that it's practically an admission of guilt?" He turned on his side so that he was facing her. "By assuming a false name and identity you're acting as if you *were* guilty of murdering Buck."

"Farrell *is* my real name, my maiden name. And so is Sharon," she returned defensively. "It was Buck who insisted on calling me Sherri because he thought Sharon sounded too middle-class. Sherri Starr is the false identity! I was never that woman with the dyed black hair, the false eyelashes, heavy makeup and those gaudy clothes. That was how Buck felt the wife of a rock star should look."

She shook her head incredulously, as if she still couldn't believe she'd ever been that person. "I went along with it to please him, to try to hold on to him when he started running around with groupies again and..." She brushed the bangs away from her face but was unable to brush away the pain darkening her eyes. "Oh, I don't want to talk about any of this."

"I'm sorry." Tenderly, Ross put his hand over the fist she held clenched in her lap. "I didn't mean to drag up more painful memories, I was just—"

"Ross, believe me, I've never been more myself than I am right now." Her fingers shifted to twine with his. "Especially when I'm with you."

"All I'm trying to say, Sharon, is that the only way you and I can start a new life together is if we both face the truth about the past so we can put it behind us forever."

"But I've told you the truth about the past!" she protested.

"That's not enough." His fingers tightened around hers. "You've got to accept Morgan's offer and acknowledge the fact that you're Buck Starr's widow."

"You don't know what you're asking me to do, Ross." She pulled her hand out of his. "I can't go through that again. You don't know what it's like being turned into a media freak." Tears filled her eyes but she fought to hold them back. "Seeing your name and face plastered all over the newspapers, the stories, all the lies, and people pointing you out everywhere you go. *That's* what I've been hiding from!"

"You can't go on hiding forever, Sharon," Ross insisted. "*Now* is the time to face them."

"No!" She turned away from him as if she'd given up hope of ever getting him to understand.

"You've got to prove to them that you're not what they thought you were." Reaching out, he grabbed her by the shoulders and turned her back to him. "I want them to see you as I do, to know what a warm, loving woman you really are."

Sharon was too deeply moved by the startling admission of Ross's love and faith in her to reply.

"What you're doing in Buck's memory," he went on, his voice thick with emotion, "is a very beautiful thing and you should let everyone know about it." His hands tightened around her shoulders and he pulled her closer to him. "*I* can help you do that."

Her eyes widened in surprise. "What do you mean? How?"

"By taking your story to the papers, the real story." Ross's mouth suddenly went dry. He drew in a long, steadying breath. "You see, I'm—"

"It wouldn't work," she cut him off. "Once you've been branded with a certain image, as I have, no one will believe anything else. You don't know what reporters are like. They'll twist everything around until the truth is distorted beyond recognition."

"You're talking about yellow journalism," he shot back defensively. "Most reporters are interested in the truth."

"The truth?" She laughed, a single, bitter laugh that cut through him like a knife; with each accusing word, the knife twisted slowly in his guts. "They don't care about the truth.

They don't even care about people. All they care about is getting a story. And they'll do anything to get it!''

Ross dropped his eyes. Slowly, he withdrew his hands.

"I don't want to see another reporter as long as I live," she finished angrily. "I despise them, every last one of them!''

Turning his face away, Ross stared out at the darkness beyond the window. All he could see was the hatred in Sharon's eyes.

"Ross, don't be angry," she pleaded, putting her hand softly on his chest. "Please try to understand how I feel."

"But I do understand." If only he could get her to understand why he'd had to do what he did. He was afraid now that she never would. "And I'm not angry, just..." He couldn't tell her that either, how utterly defeated he felt, and ashamed.

Tenderly, Sharon ran her hand over Ross's chest. "I've never been as happy as I am with you." Her fingers burrowed into the tawny curls, seeking the feel and warmth of his skin. "Can you blame me for not wanting to let anything spoil such happiness?''

Ross turned back to Sharon and the knife twisted inside him one more time when he saw the look of naked love on her face. The thought of never seeing that look again tore him up. His hands reached out to frame her face, as if her love for him were a physical thing he could actually hold in his hands, and as long as he could hold it, he would never lose it.

"I love you, Sharon. No matter what happens, I want you to remember that. I've never loved anyone the way I love you." His mouth took hers in a kiss that was filled more with pain than pleasure. She wrapped herself around him, giving herself up to him without restraint. His kiss deepened, his hunger for her growing instead of lessening. He kissed her until they were both shaking in each other's arms.

"Everything's going to be all right, Ross, you'll see," Sharon said breathlessly when she'd dragged her mouth from his. "As long as we love each other the past can't hurt us anymore."

From the depths of his soul, Ross prayed that Sharon's wish might be true even though he knew that the past wasn't through with them yet; not until he told her who he really was. But for the moment all he could do, all he wanted to do was forget everything and lose himself in the blinding ecstasy he'd known only with her.

As he pulled her on top of him, his mouth reaching hungrily for hers, he silently vowed that he'd find a way to make her wish come true.

"Ross, look! The swans are back," Sharon cried, pointing to the pair of exquisite creatures gliding elegantly over the water beside the pier, their smooth white feathers gleaming in the sun.

"As long as you keep feeding them, they'll keep coming back for more," said Ross with a smile as he followed her out of the cabin.

"Oh, I hope so." Her eyes glowed with excitement, and her skin still held a rosy trace of their early morning lovemaking. "They're so beautiful."

"So are you." Ross was amazed to find desire beginning to stir in him again. His eyes moved possessively over her body; the summery halter dress she wore was no barrier to his memories. "You look like a swan in that white dress."

She laughed. "Are you sure you don't mean a chicken?"

"Not with that neck." His fingers traced the long delicate curve of her neck, her bare shoulder and slender arm. "Definitely a swan."

"*You* look like a cat," said Sharon, looking up into his yellow eyes. Her hand went up to brush a tawny eyebrow and caress the lean, stark lines of his face. "A sleek and slightly dangerous jungle cat." She laughed again as her fingers playfully ruffled his hair, which was still damp from the shower they'd shared. "We make a rather odd couple, wouldn't you say? A swan and a jungle cat?"

"No," he purred, his eyes darkening to the color of burnt gold. "I think we make a great couple."

A thrill went through Sharon, as it always did when she saw the love and desire in Ross's eyes, and suddenly she was reluctant to leave him for even a few hours. She twined her arms lightly around his neck. "Are you sure I can't talk you into going into town with me?"

He sighed reluctantly. "I really have to get some work done. I'm way behind schedule as it is."

"But it's such a beautiful day." She gestured, indicating the sun blazing high in a cobalt-blue sky, shimmering on the water; the long-delayed summer had finally arrived. "I hate to think of you all cooped up with dull legal briefs on such a lovely day. Can't you work tonight?"

A smile played on his lips. "I'd rather save tonight for you."

She laughed softly, throatily. "Has anyone ever told you that you're insatiable?"

"No. I've never been insatiable before."

"I know the feeling," Sharon murmured, her arms tightening around his neck. "But if you keep talking that way, you won't get any work done this afternoon either."

He grinned. "*Now* who's being insatiable?"

"You started."

"And I intend to finish what I started when you get back." Bending his head, he sealed his promise with a kiss. For an instant he was tempted to go with her, then he remembered that he couldn't risk being seen with her in town; too many people knew him. He stepped out of her embrace. "How long will you be gone?"

"The rest of the afternoon," said Sharon, starting reluctantly toward her car. "I want to check out all the antique stores in town. Will that give you enough time to work?"

"Plenty."

"I'll pick up some groceries," she added when she'd slipped behind the wheel of the Jaguar convertible and started up the motor. "We're out of food. Is there anything in particular you'd like?"

"No...uhh, yes," he amended impulsively. "I'd like some ice cream. Strawberry swirl."

"Strawberry swirl?" She laughed incredulously. "You're kidding."

"No. I have a real weakness for strawberry swirl." He leaned over the top of the car door. "It tastes almost as sweet and delicious as you do." Swiftly, he bent his head and took her mouth; his tongue slipped inside to take a long, thorough taste of her. When he lifted his head, his eyes were burnt gold again. "Hurry back."

"Yes," she breathed.

His hands gripped the top of the car door for a moment longer, as if he meant to hold her back physically, before dropping slowly to his sides. "Drive carefully now, you hear?"

"Yes, of course," she assured him, shifting into first. "Good luck with your work," she called out to him as she backed out of the driveway. When she turned on to the main road, she waved and honked her horn as a last goodbye.

Ross watched until the sleek white sports car disappeared around the bend in the road. He remembered how much fun they'd had that time he'd shown her around Baltimore and he wished he could have gone with her again. All that would change very soon, he promised himself, as he walked back to the cabin and the article that was locked in his desk, waiting to be finished.

Everything would change once the article on Buck was published. Once Sharon read it, she would have to understand why he'd had to do what he'd done to her, and why he still kept his real identity a secret. He'd tried to tell her the truth several times in the two weeks since their talk but his fear of losing her had always stopped him. He'd watched her love for him deepen more and more each day; his love for her went so deep it scared him sometimes. The emotional desert his life had been before he knew her was as unreal as a dream to him now, and he couldn't imagine his life without her.

Ross's hands were tense when he unlocked the rolltop desk and opened the folder containing the rough copy of the article. Slowly, objectively he went over the article, trying to see it through Sharon's eyes. Picking up his pen, he went over it again, word for word, determined to make it still clearer, even more precise. How could she fail to understand?

Sharon was on her way back home, a large bag of groceries propped up on the seat next to hers, when she saw the hand-painted sign pointing to an antique store situated off the main road. She'd meant just to drive past the store to see if it was worth another trip to town, but the sight of the wicker table and chairs sitting out on the lawn prompted her to stop.

The table and chairs would make a perfect gift for Ross once she refinished them; they were just what he needed for his back porch. Pulling into the driveway, Sharon jumped impulsively out of her car and hurried inside. The barnlike interior of the store was filled to the rafters with a chaotic assortment of antiques. It took her a moment to locate the owner; the woman was busy dusting a collection of duck decoys.

"How much do you want for the wicker table and chairs out front?" Sharon called over to her.

The tall, thin woman, who appeared to be in her forties, turned to look over at her. Her shrewd, dark eyes took in Sharon's appearance as if she were an item she was considering purchasing for the store. "The wicker table an' those matchin' chairs?" she repeated with a pronounced Southern accent. Her gaze shifted to the open doorway to evaluate the classic Jaguar idling in the driveway. "Two hundred dollars for the table, an' a hundred a piece for the chairs."

"They're pretty beat-up looking," Sharon protested.

"We just sell 'em, we don't recondition 'em," she returned, her tone implying that making a sale was completely unimportant to her. "If you want 'em, you'll have to take 'em as they are, beat-up an' all."

"I'll give you three hundred dollars for the lot."

"Three-fifty."

"Three hundred," Sharon insisted. "I'm sure that's more than you ever expected to make on them."

"I don't take credit cards," the woman grumbled, dropping the feather duster into a dented brass pot before she started toward the counter.

"Will you take a check?"

She pursed her thin lips. "You from around here?"

"Yes."

She shrugged and reached for a pen and her receipt book. "All rightie. Make the check out to Eastern Shore Antiques."

"I'll never get the table and chairs in my car," Sharon told her as she began making out the check. "Can you deliver them?"

"That'll be another ten dollars."

"All right."

"Can't deliver 'em today. You'll have to wait till tomorrow." She didn't bother to ask Sharon if that was convenient for her. "What's your name and address?"

"Sharon Farrell. Crabman's Cove. White Egret Road."

The woman looked up from the bill. "Why, that's the old Huntley place!"

"Huntley?" Sharon repeated while she tore the check along its perforated edge. The name rang a bell, somehow, but she couldn't quite place it.

The woman leaned across the counter, her eyes coming alive with interest. "Tell me, is R.B. still stayin' at the cabin? No one's seen him around all summer."

"R.B.?" Sharon's hand froze as she was replacing her checkbook in her purse. Suddenly, she remembered where she'd seen that name.

The owner's attitude turned friendly. "R.B. Huntley? Haven't you met him yet?" She laughed, a low sexy laugh. "You'd sure remember him if you had. R.B. Hunkley is what most of the girls around here call him. Why, he's got the cabin right next to your place."

"No!" Sharon cried, her mind refusing to deal with the implications of what she was hearing. "That cabin belongs to Ross Baxter."

"That's him," the woman insisted cheerfully. "Ross Baxter Huntley. But folks around here have been callin' him R.B. ever since he was a kid."

Sharon had to grab the edge of the counter with both hands to steady herself. "You mean, he's the R.B. Huntley who writes for the *Baltimore Examiner*?"

"That's the one."

Sharon gasped but no sound came out. She felt as if she'd just been punched in the stomach. "I have to go now," she heard herself say in a high, thin voice. Somehow, her feet moved without any conscious effort on her part.

"Hang on," the store owner exclaimed, waving a slip of paper as she came rushing out from behind the counter. "You've gone an' forgot your copy of the receipt."

"Thank you," Sharon murmured absently as the receipt was shoved into her hand.

"I'll have the boy deliver your goods sometime tomorrow afternoon," she called out from the doorway.

But Sharon didn't hear her as she slid behind the wheel of her car, the crumpled receipt slipping unseen out of her hand onto the floor. Nor was she aware of her surroundings as she drove past the quaint little shops and restaurants that lined the town's main street, down the country road that led home and past the endless rows of corn stalks ripening in the summer sun. She was still on automatic pilot when she pulled into her driveway.

Ross's head shot up when he heard the familiar sound of tires crunching gravel. Quickly, he pulled the page that he was retyping out of the typewriter and dropped it on top of the finished pages. He had just enough time to pull the roll-top down over his desk when Sharon entered the cabin.

Eleven

Unable to move another step, Sharon came to a halt a few feet past the door. A strange numbness continued to suffuse her body, a sense of unreality still clouded her mind. She was vaguely aware of a growing chill inside her as if the warm blood were being slowly drained from her veins. All she could do was watch as Ross stepped away from his desk.

The oddest thought suddenly struck her: she was in love with a man who didn't exist. Yet this man who was really someone else had the same fiercely intelligent eyes as her lover, the same tawny hair that felt like silk between her fingers, the sensuous mouth that gave her so much pleasure and always cried out her name at the moment of ecstasy. She recognized the eagerness in his step as he hurried toward her, his face glowing with the joy of seeing her. She was sure now that it was all a misunderstanding; the store owner had to have meant someone else.

"What took you so long?" he asked, wrapping a strong, possessive arm around her shoulders. "I missed you." He dropped a kiss on top of her head and hugged her to his side.

"I thought you needed the time to... work." The chill began sinking into her bones. Fearfully, she looked over at his desk. The corner of a page of white typing paper stuck out between the edges of the wood, curling upward as if the rolltop had been slammed down on it abruptly. "Did you get your work done?"

"I don't even want to think about work now that you're back," he replied evasively. "I was just about to get myself a glass of beer. Would you like one, too?"

Sharon managed a quick nod. Ross gave her shoulders an impulsive squeeze before he released her to stride to the kitchen.

It seemed to Sharon that the corner of the white typing paper was like a powerful magnet pulling her over to the desk against her will. The rattling sound the rolltop made as she slid it out of view came from somewhere far away. Unconsciously, she uncrimped the corner of the typing page as she picked it up and started to read.

Ross's hands tightened around the beer mugs and he came to a shocked standstill in the doorway when he caught sight of Sharon reading the article, a look of growing horror on her face.

Sharon heard his sharp intake of breath clear across the room. Slowly, she turned her head and looked over at him. "It's true, isn't it?" she said as if she still couldn't bring herself to believe it even though she was holding the evidence right in her hand. "You're R.B. Huntley... the reporter. You're the one who's writing the article on Buck's death for *The Examiner*."

"Sharon, I—"

"I know it's true," she said, her voice unnaturally calm, "but I want to hear you say it."

The guilt twisting the rugged lines of his face, holding him motionless in the doorway, was as clear an admission as his faltering words. "Yes . . . it's true."

The page slid out of Sharon's hand and fluttered slowly down to the floor as she stared at Ross as though she'd never seen him before. He'd suddenly become a stranger to her. A stranger to whom she'd revealed her most secret thoughts and feelings. A stranger who'd explored every inch of her body with a sensual intimacy she'd never known. She'd taken a stranger deep inside her body, into her very heart and soul!

Suddenly, the icy numbness, which had been like a protective shield around her, vanished and there was no defense against the pain of betrayal that twisted through her until she could barely breathe. "How could you do such a thing just to get a lousy story?" With one angry motion, she swept the rest of the neatly stacked pages off his desk, sending them flying in all directions.

Her violent movement somehow freed Ross as well. He set the beer mugs down on the first convenient spot just as she sent the research folder flying.

Sharon gasped as she made out the items littering the floor at her feet—old newspaper clippings and pictures of her, a police photo of Buck's dead body, and one of the gun with a handwritten tag on it, a copy of the postmortem report that even she had never seen—all the broken pieces of her life. "What kind of a man are you that you could do such a thing?"

Ross halted a few feet away from her. He wanted to reach out and take her in his arms but the look of outrage he saw in her eyes stopped him. "Sharon, I can explain."

"How can you explain away what's so obvious? You set me up right from the start. You came here, pretending to be someone else, just to get a story. You even pretended to love me, and you used my feelings to get me to open up to you." Tears burned behind her eyes but she refused to shed them. "I told you things I would never have told another human being as long as I lived!"

"Sharon, I never *pretended* to love you, I *do* love you," Ross insisted. "You're right about everything else, but I never used you. I never even meant for us to become lovers because—"

She put her hand up to stop him as if she couldn't handle another devastating revelation. "No, don't tell me." Slowly, her hand sank to her side. "I already know what you're going to say anyway." She took a long, deep breath and let it out in anguished shreds. "You're married."

"No, I'm not," he assured her, moving a step closer. "I've never been married."

She stepped back. "Then the story you told me about your wife being shot to death was just another lie?"

"Yes," he admitted unashamedly.

"But why?"

"Because I had to find a way to get you to trust me." His tone made it clear that he felt perfectly justified in what he'd done. "I knew you would have to identify with someone whose spouse had also been shot to death, and it would make it easier for you to relate to me."

"Relate to you?" she repeated bitterly. "I hurt for you, deeply, because I knew from experience what you must have been going through. And you used that?" Shaking her head in disgust, she turned and walked away from him, stepping over several clippings as she did.

"Sharon, you've got to understand something," Ross persisted, coming after her. "It's true that I had to lie to you. And I did set you up. But it was only because I was convinced you'd murdered your husband."

Sharon stiffened but she went on walking over to the living room area without looking at him. "So *you* believed those stories in the papers, too?"

"It wasn't just the stories," Ross said, quickening his step to keep pace with her angry strides. "I knew you'd signed a premarital agreement and in case of a divorce you'd have ended up with a minor settlement. But if your husband were to die, you stood to inherit his entire estate."

She stopped abruptly in front of the couch and spun around to face him. "You thought I killed him for the money?"

"Yes. Buck *was* planning to divorce you," Ross pointed out. "He told me himself the last time I saw him."

She shook her head impatiently. "Buck said a lot of things when he was on—" Her voice broke off; it was a moment before she could speak again. "You knew Buck?"

"Yes, I knew him," Ross said evenly. "He was my brother, Sharon."

"Your brother?" What he'd just told her was so preposterous she almost laughed, until she looked up into his eyes—eyes the same startling shade of amber as Buck's— and she knew he was telling the truth. She laughed then, a short, bitter laugh. "Lying obviously runs in your family. He never told me he had a brother."

"Buck ran away from home when he was seventeen and never looked back," Ross explained. "He changed his name, his whole life-style. I hadn't seen him in almost ten years when I read in the papers about his drug problems so I got in touch with him. I was hoping there was something I could do to help him but..." Sighing, he raked his hand through his hair. "Anyway, that's when he told me that *you* were the cause of all his problems and that he'd be okay once he divorced you. He told me you were doing everything to wreck his career including sleeping with the other members of his band. He was convinced you were out to get him."

"But I told you he suffered from paranoid delusions when he was strung out!"

"I didn't know that then. I didn't even realize how sick he really was or..." His voice trailed off, guilt darkening his eyes. "Anyway, a couple of weeks later he was dead."

"But why didn't you get in touch with me then?" Sharon demanded. "I would have been able to explain everything."

Ross laughed harshly. "After the stories Buck told me about you, do you think I would have believed anything you said?"

"No, of course not."

"Sharon, I didn't come here just to get a story," Ross said bluntly. "I came here to find proof or to make you confess that you'd deliberately murdered Buck."

"I didn't murder him!" she cried desperately. "But the gun is the only proof there is that... oh, my God!" Slowly, she sank down onto the couch. "How could I have been so stupid? The gun you tried to give me, that was a set-up too, wasn't it?" She didn't need to wait for his answer; it was written all over his face. "I should have realized your having the exact same gun was too much of a coincidence. But how could I know you were capable of doing such a thing?" she asked, almost talking to herself.

"I couldn't think of any other way to find out the truth about Buck's death," Ross resumed, sitting down beside her on the couch. "I was beginning to have doubts about your murdering him but I couldn't understand why you were still in hiding. Or why you had so much guilt about his death you couldn't even talk about it. I was sure that if you saw the gun again, actually held it in your hands, you would finally break down and confess the truth."

"And you were right," said Sharon, her voice as cold and hard as her feelings toward him. "But you never stopped to consider how much pain that would cause me."

"I wasn't concerned about your feelings," Ross admitted impatiently. "I thought you'd murdered my brother!"

"Do you still think I murdered him?"

"No, of course not." Ross's face softened and regret mingled with guilt in his eyes. Reaching over, he took her hand in his. "I'm sorry. I didn't realize how much you'd suffered because of Buck's death. If I had, I could never have done what I did to you."

Sharon hardened herself against his soft words, his warm, seductive tone; she let her hand rest limply in his, unaffected by his touch. "What if you'd found out that I *had* murdered him instead? What would you have done then?"

Ross was forced to think about that for a moment. "I don't know," he admitted finally. "I was already so much in love with you, I don't know what I would have done."

Sharon pulled her hand away. "You love me and yet you went on lying to me all these weeks?"

"I tried to tell you the truth the night we had that talk about the competition," he assured her. "I started to tell you who I was but you wouldn't let me. When you told me how much you hated reporters, I knew if I told you then you would hate me too." He leaned toward her in an attempt to get through to her and she caught a whiff of the musky scent she'd come to know so well. "So I decided to wait until—"

"Until you could finish meting out your own special brand of punishment?" she cut him off bitterly. "Getting me to expose my past wasn't enough for you. You had to get me to expose myself as a woman in the most intimate way possible!"

"No! I just wanted to wait until—"

"Until I was so much in love with you I would be completely devastated when I found out what you were really up to?"

"I couldn't tell you because I was afraid of losing you," Ross protested. "I love you, Sharon. I do."

She had to look away from the despair in his eyes, which left her shaken and confused. Only by reminding herself how convincingly he'd played his part all those weeks was she able to think objectively again. "You were afraid of losing a good story, you mean," she said coldly, staring down at the rug. "Why else would you have kept on lying to me?"

"But I didn't lie to you," he insisted, "not in any real sense." He slid his hand into her hair and turned her face back to his. "I may not have told you who I was, but I was never more myself than when I was with you. You must know that, Sharon." When she didn't, couldn't speak he searched for the answer in her eyes. His fingers tightened as, inexorably, he drew her face to within a breath of his. "I know it's ironic under the circumstances, but I've never been so open with a woman before or so completely honest in my feelings."

He lowered his head, seeking her lips. Before he could find them and work his sensual magic, Sharon pulled her head away, breaking his hold on her.

Ross's hand clenched into a fist and he slammed it down on the sofa cushion in frustration. "Why won't you believe me?"

"How *can* I believe you," Sharon cried miserably, jumping to her feet, "when everything you've ever told me is a lie!"

"That's not true!"

"Lies and tricks, all of it! To get a *story*!"

Ross's hand shot out to grab Sharon's arm and stop her from walking away from him. "Then what the hell am I still doing here?" With one hard tug, he pulled her back down on the couch beside him. "I'd gotten all the information I needed weeks ago. If a story was all I was after, I'd have taken off once I got it."

"But you didn't get the story you were after," she accused, struggling to twist free of his grasp. "You could have been looking for more evidence."

Grabbing her free arm, Ross pinned her against the back of the sofa, making it impossible for her to get away from him, to do anything but deal with him directly. "Sharon, I swear to you," he said, his voice raw, "I may have had hidden reasons for coming here but the only reason I'm here now is because I want to be with you." He searched her face intensely to see if he was finally getting through to her. "I love you. You've got to believe me."

"How can I?"

"Dammit!" Ross finally exploded in frustration. "Do you think I wanted to fall in love with you...the woman who killed my brother?" His fingers dug into her arms almost painfully. "I thought I hated you. For three years I thought I hated you and then I met you and you weren't anything like I'd expected you to be. You were like no woman I'd ever known."

He laughed suddenly, harshly, his breath brushing her stunned face. "You'll never know how hard I tried not to love you. But every time I looked at you, I wanted you. And every time I wanted you, I felt I was betraying my brother's memory. Until it got to the point where I wanted you so much I didn't even care about Buck anymore." With an almost angry motion, he pulled her up against him. "All I cared about was you," he grated, his mouth coming down hard on hers.

His arms went around her back, surrounding her, while his mouth moved on hers with a hunger born of desperation. She sought to pull away at first but he wouldn't let go. He kissed her until she was shaking in his arms and he was shaking as much as she was.

Suddenly, his hands slid down to her hips to press them intimately against his. "You don't think I could fake *that*, do you?" A shiver went through her when she felt the warm, hard proof of his desire through the layers of their clothing. "I couldn't fake that if I wanted to." His hands glided up to her breasts and quickly found the swollen tips. "Any more than *your* body can hide how much you want me."

Swiftly, he bent his head to capture one of the taut peaks straining against her halter top. Through the light cotton fabric he tugged at her with barely controlled hunger, sending melting waves of pleasure washing over her, waves she could drown in so easily if she let herself.

"Ross, don't . . ." Sharon cried, pressing her trembling hands against his shoulders to push him away; lean, hard muscles contracted at her touch.

"It's all right," he murmured soothingly when he'd lifted his mouth from her. "Everything's going to be all right now." He dropped a kiss in the exposed hollow between her breasts before he looked up at her, his eyes like molten gold.

"I'm so glad everything's finally out in the open. Now we can put the past behind us for good and start a new life together." His low, deep voice moved over her like the intoxicating warmth his fingers were trailing along the undercurve of her breasts. "Marry me, Sharon, and I promise I'll spend the rest of our lives making it up to you for any hurt I've caused you." With soft little kisses he closed her burning eyelids. "Once the article comes out, we can—"

"What?" Her eyes flew open, breaking the sensual web he'd spun so expertly around her. "You mean...you're still planning on publishing the article?"

"Yes, of course." He sounded surprised that she would think otherwise. His hands never stopped their tantalizing movements.

Pushing away from him, Sharon staggered to her feet. "Even though you know how I feel about it and...and that it's going to ruin my life again?"

"No, it won't. Just the opposite," he insisted with a knowing smile. "Sharon, you've got to face the truth. We'll face it together." With one sure motion he was on his feet before her. "It won't be as difficult as you think." His hand reached out to touch her reassuringly; she took no notice.

"I was right about you," she accused him bitterly. "The story is all you really care about."

"That's not true," Ross protested, "and once you read it, you'll know what I'm talking about." He turned and headed for the study where the typewritten pages were strewn all over the floor. "I want you to read it right now so—"

"I don't want to read it!" Sharon cried furiously as she brushed past him, pages crackling under her heels. "I never want to read it! And I never want to see you again!"

For a moment, Ross was too stunned to move; he caught up with Sharon just as she reached the door. "What are you going to do now?" he demanded. "Run away again?"

"Yes! As far away from you as I can get!"

"You can't go on running the rest of your life, Sharon."

"I will if it means getting away from people like you," she snapped, pulling open the door. "People who make a living exploiting the tragedies of others."

"I've never exploited you or anyone in my life," Ross countered, his voice savage. "All I've ever cared about is finding the truth."

"The truth?" Sharon turned slowly in the doorway and stared at him incredulously for a moment. "You still don't see what you did to me, do you, Ross? You're still right. And as self-righteous as ever."

"What are you talking about?"

"You feel completely justified in doing what you did to me because it was all done in the name of truth or justice or some other bloodless ideal. But you never cared about what your idealism would cost me in pain." Refusing to give him the satisfaction of seeing her cry, she blinked back the tears stinging her eyes. "I trusted you as I haven't been able to trust anyone in years. And you used that to get your story."

"Sharon, I—"

"You got me to open up to you, to love you. You knew I loved you so much I'd be miserable without you...." Her voice cracked and she had to take a long, deep breath before she could go on. "You counted on that to get me to accept what you'd done. And *that's* what I'll never be able to forgive you. Never!"

Through a mist of tears, Sharon saw the look of bewilderment on Ross's face before she slammed her way out of the cabin where she'd spent the happiest moments of her

life. Her throat ached from the sobs she refused to give in to.
She was afraid that if she started crying now she would never
stop. By the time she'd finished packing a suitcase and made
a hotel reservation in Baltimore, the tears were frozen inside her.

But as she was about to get into her car, she noticed the
bag of groceries on the other seat. She'd forgotten all about
them. The lovely dinner she'd planned for that evening had
to be spoiled from sitting out in the hot sun for so long. The
strawberry swirl ice cream had already melted, and was
oozing out of its carton all over the other groceries. Tears
were streaming down Sharon's face when she dumped the
groceries into the garbage.

While he watched Sharon's car disappear around the bend
in the road, Ross knocked back the stiffest drink he'd ever
made. He continued to drink and stare out the window until it was too dark to see, and he was too drunk to feel anything.

Twelve

Mrs. Starr is here, Sam," the secretary, who'd just escorted Sharon from the reception room into the glass and wood office, announced casually before shutting the door behind her.

Sharon was surprised that a secretary would call her boss by what was obviously a nickname, but one look at the woman sitting behind the desk told her that the editor of the *Examiner's Sunday Magazine* was not your average boss. With her impeccably tailored suit, and every ash-blond hair in place, she made a strange contrast with the mind-boggling clutter on her desk. Yet, somehow, Sharon felt sure the editor knew where every last scrap of paper was located should she need it.

Without looking up, she finished scrawling an okay on the rough layout she'd been examining when Sharon had come in. She gave the impression of being annoyed at the inter-

ruption—as if Sharon had been the one who'd forced this
meeting and not the other way around!

"So you're Sherri Starr," she said bluntly, getting to her
feet. With impatient, long-legged strides, she covered the
distance between them. "I'm Samantha Carson." She ex-
tended an imperious hand. "I'm glad you changed your
mind about coming to see me."

Reluctantly, Sharon returned the handshake. It was a
brisk, no-nonsense handshake, as direct as the pale-gray
gaze that was moving over her. "I'm not here because I want
to be, Ms. Carson."

Samantha Carson smiled as if she preferred honesty to
mere politeness. "You're certainly not what I expected," she
admitted when she finished her examination. "But then,
that's exactly what R.B. said after he met you." A thin,
arched eyebrow went up when she saw Sharon stiffen at the
mere mention of Ross. "A very classy-looking lady was how
he put it as I recall."

"Ms. Carson, I—"

"Call me Sam," she ordered, waving Sharon over to the
suede armchair in front of her desk. "Everybody does."

"I prefer to stand," Sharon returned coolly. "What I
have to say won't take long."

"You've changed your mind about the interview?" She
didn't wait for Sharon's answer but turned and walked
briskly over to one of the windows that offered a four-sided
view of the sprawling copy room outside.

"No. As I told your secretary, I have no intention of
doing an interview for your paper."

The editor pulled the cord on the venetian blind, closing
the slats; she caught the questioniong look on Sharon's face.
"When the blinds are closed, my secretary doesn't put any
calls through or allow anyone in my office," she explained

matter-of-factly before continuing to the next window. "Now we can talk without being disturbed."

"I didn't come here to discuss this matter," Sharon insisted, "but to tell you what I intend to do about it." She was forced to keep turning in order to follow the editor's progress around the room, closing the blinds as she went. "Your secretary has informed me that if I don't agree to the interview, you intend doing a celebrity profile on me anyway...without my cooperation."

"I'd prefer to do it *with* your cooperation," Sam Carson said sharply on her way back to her desk. "Hell, it's to *your* advantage, not ours."

"*My* advantage?"

"I would think you'd jump at the chance to finally tell your side of the story."

Sharon laughed bitterly. "Since when has the press been interested in *my* side of the story?"

Warmth suddenly suffused Sam's pale-gray eyes. "I know you got a raw deal the first time around. These last three years must have been very hard on you." Her voice was soft with concern and it threw Sharon completely. "But don't sell us *all* short!" she snapped, quickly reverting to her usual manner. She threw herself into the suede swivel chair behind her desk and reached for her cigarettes. "Come on over here and sit down."

It was an order, not an invitation, but Sharon had gotten a glimpse of the vulnerability behind Samantha Carson's brusque facade and suddenly, she couldn't dislike the woman quite as much as she had. Maybe she was amenable to reason after all, Sharon hoped, as she seated herself.

"I'm glad you changed your mind about coming to see me." Sam exhaled a long stream of smoke. "Because—"

"How did you know where to find me?" Sharon broke in.

"Mr. Morgan of The School of Performing Arts sent us a press release about the Buck Starr Competition that's going to be held next Saturday," she explained quickly, as if impatient to get on to other things. "I told him we were planning on covering the event and needed more background information on your husband. He was only too delighted to give me the name of the hotel you've been staying at these past two weeks."

"Does Ross know where I'm staying?" Sharon blurted out before she could stop herself.

"Yes. I told him myself."

"I see." Sharon stared down at the handbag she hadn't realized she was clutching in her lap. If he really loved her, she thought miserably, he would have made an attempt to get in touch with her. She'd been right about him, after all.

"Sharon—may I call you Sharon?" Sam asked then rushed on before Sharon could give her consent. "What made you change your mind about giving out the awards?"

"I've had a lot of time to think these last few weeks," Sharon admitted. "I guess I finally realized that I couldn't keep running away for the rest of my life. That in the end I was only running away from myself."

A pale, arched eyebrow went up. "Then you're not leaving Baltimore as you'd planned?"

"No. I like it here. I've made a new home for myself," Sharon said proudly, "and I'm not going to allow other people to force me to give it up. I'm going to fight back this time." She sat up in her chair. "And that's what I came here to tell you. I'm prepared to fight your newspaper, too, if I have to. I've already spoken to a lawyer."

"A lawyer?" Sam sounded more amused than concerned.

"Yes. Now, he's informed me that there's nothing I can do about the article you've already published in last Sunday's magazine section but—"

"Have you read it?"

"No."

"I didn't think so. You should read it." Swiveling around, she picked up a copy of the magazine from one of the low metal cabinets lining the wall behind her desk. "Here." She handed it across the desk to Sharon. "I saved you a copy."

Sharon pulled back in her seat. "I don't want it."

She dropped the magazine on top of a stack of papers directly in front of Sharon. "It's one of the best articles R.B.'s ever written."

"I'm sure it is," Sharon returned sarcastically. "I'll just have to take your word for it. My lawyer read it and he claims I have no case because everything you printed is based on actual fact. But if you were to publish an article on me, personally, repeating the lies and stories about me that had been invented when—"

"*The Baltimore Examiner* is not a scandal sheet!" the editor cut her off sharply, her professional pride clearly stung. "If you'd read R.B.'s article you'd know that." She squashed out her cigarette in the ashtray. "That's why I'd chosen *him* to write this series. Most reporters would have gone for the sensational elements in the story while *his* first concern is always the human element. If you knew anything about the man—"

"I didn't come here to discuss Ross...uhh, Mr. Huntley," Sharon interrupted; it was a subject that still caused her too much pain. "I came here to discuss the article."

"Hell, whether you do the article or not is immaterial to me," Sam Carson snapped. She sat up in her chair. "May I be blunt?"

Sharon had to smile in spite of herself. "What have you been up to now?"

"That's always been one of my problems," Sam admitted with a wry laugh. For a moment, Sharon actually liked the woman; she certainly had to admire her honesty. "The article was just an excuse to get you to see me," the editor went on, reaching for another cigarette. "It's R.B. I really want to talk to you about." She glared accusingly at Sharon. "What the hell have you done to that man?"

Sharon gasped. "What have *I* done to *him*?"

"I've known the man for almost seven years and I've never seen him in such a state. He's been wandering around here like one of the walking wounded." She pointed the cigarette she'd forgotten to light accusingly at Sharon. "Why are you doing this to him? Don't you know that the man is crazy in love for you?"

"No," Sharon murmured ruefully, "I don't know that. If he loved me he wouldn't have lied to me or tricked me just to get a story."

"It had nothing to do with the story," Sam insisted. "Before he met you, R.B. was convinced you'd murdered his brother."

"I know. I've gone through all that with him already."

"Did you know that he blames himself for his brother's death?"

"No," Sharon breathed. "Why?"

"I don't know how much R.B.'s told you about his relationship with Buck but it was a rather complex one." Sam paused finally to light her cigarette. "As the eldest son, R.B. was his parents' favorite, and he always did everything his parents expected of him. Buck, on the other hand, was always getting into trouble, ever since he was a child." The tip glowed as she took a quick puff. "It was probably the only way he could get his parents' attention. He knew he could never get their approval. I've met his parents. They're good people but very strict. Their high moral code couldn't have been easy to live up to."

"I always wondered why Buck married someone like me, despising middle-class values the way he did," Sharon found herself admitting. "Maybe that's why he tried to turn me into something I wasn't."

"Ever since they were kids, R.B. was always covering up for Buck," Sam went on, "always trying to get him out of trouble. I think he sensed what made Buck act the way he did." She flicked the ash off her cigarette. "I know no one was happier than he when Buck became a big success. But when he started getting into trouble with drugs, R.B. rushed to L.A. to try to help him. He couldn't, as you know, and when he came back he acted as if he'd failed him."

Sam took a long, thoughtful drag on her cigarette before she continued. "I think he actually believed that if he'd tried harder he might have saved Buck. But since he wasn't able to save him, he would at least punish the person responsible for his death—you."

Sharon nodded, pain darkening her eyes. "He chose a very effective punishment."

"But he really believed all those stories about you," Sam went on, leaning across the desk toward her. "He was convinced you'd murdered his brother. In that light, is what he did so difficult to understand?"

"No," Sharon assured her. "I do understand that part of it. What I can't understand is how he could go on lying to me afterward."

"Afterward?"

"After we became lovers," she admitted unashamedly.

Sam sighed, breathing out a heavy stream of smoke. "Well, it's certainly not like him. If anything, R.B.'s almost brutally honest." She smiled wryly. "An unfortunate trait we both share. So if he didn't tell you the truth about himself, it had to be because he was afraid of losing you." She took one last drag on her cigarette, then put it out. "And he was right, wasn't he?"

Sharon was unable to answer.

"Do you still love him, Sharon?"

"What difference does it make if I love him?" she asked miserably. "You can't have love without trust. How will I ever be able to trust him again?"

"If you love him enough, you'll find a way."

"But if *he* really loved me, he would never have published that article," Sharon protested. "He knew how much it would hurt me but he did it anyway."

"He did it *because* he loved you, Sharon," Sam insisted. "If you'd read the article you'd know that."

"What do you mean?"

"Because instead of rehashing gossip, R.B. proved your innocence," she explained. "He showed how unfairly you'd been treated by the media, how they'd used innuendo to destroy your credibility and reputation."

"Did he really do that?" Sharon murmured incredulously.

"Yes." Pushing away from her desk, Sam got to her feet. "Take a look at this," she ordered, waving Sharon over to the cabinets behind her desk. "This is another reason why I wanted you to come here."

"What is it?" Sharon asked.

"Letters," she replied, indicating the large cardboard box on top of the cabinets. "These are some of the thousands of letters we've received from the public since the article was published. These, which we haven't opened, are addressed to you."

"More hate mail?"

"No, just the opposite," Sam assured her. "Over ninety percent of the letters we received are in your favor. People writing in to say how sorry they are about what happened to you. Many of them want to know where you are now and what's become of you."

"You mean Ross didn't reveal my identity or where I'm living now?"

"Of course not," Sam said, clearly appalled at the idea. "But it wouldn't matter if he had. Because of R.B.'s article public opinion is on *your* side now." She smiled warmly, hopefully. "Do you still believe he doesn't love you?"

Emotion tightened Sharon's throat, making it impossible for her to answer. Before she could recover, the intercom buzzed.

With one quick, efficient movement, Sam picked up the receiver and pushed the flashing button. "Yes?" She tapped her foot impatiently while she listened to the speaker at the other end. "Ask him to wait. I'll be with him in a few minutes." She hung up the receiver but kept her hand on it. "Didn't R.B. tell you about the article?"

"Yes, he tried to," Sharon got out with difficulty, "but I was too angry and upset to listen."

"Then how about giving him another chance? Would you like to see him again?"

"Yes," Sharon admitted, blinking back tears.

Sam picked up the receiver with one hand and pushed the intercom button with the other. "Susan? You can send R.B. in now."

Sharon froze. So did Ross when he entered the office and saw her.

"He didn't know a thing about this. This was my idea," Sam muttered under her breath. Flashing Sharon a warm smile, she turned abruptly and made for the door. "Someone to see you, R.B.," she snapped. "But don't take your time about it. I need the office." With an imperious toss of her head, she swept past him. "Somebody's got to get some work done around here today."

The click the door made as it was shut reverberated in the stunned silence that hung between them.

Ross was the first to recover. "I know why you're here," he said, his voice tight. "Susan was just telling me about the interview." His face looked drawn and the lines etching his mouth seemed deeper than she remembered. "I could swear to you that it wasn't my idea but I'm sure you wouldn't believe me."

Sharon was so happy to see him again she could barely breathe. She was shaking inside, that uncontrollable shaking she'd known only when he touched her. "No, uhh . . . Sam and I were just discussing the *other* article; the one you wrote."

A wild kind of hope flared inside Ross and he took a step forward. "Have you read it?"

"No," Sharon admitted, "but—"

"No, why should you?" he cut her off grimly. "Well, at least I got the chance to see you one last time so I could tell you you were right," he told the carpet. "I know that now. There's no excuse for what I did to you." He looked up at her then, despair in his eyes. "I know you'll never be able to forgive me, Sharon, but neither will I."

Sharon's eyes widened in amazement and her lips parted, soft and unbearably sensuous. She was so lovely, it hurt Ross to look at her. He wheeled around and pulled the door open.

"Oh, you'll be happy to know I've joined the human race," he tossed ruefully over his shoulder. "For the first time in my life I know what it feels like to be deeply ashamed of something I've done."

Before Sharon could speak, Ross was out the door. In a daze, she caught the startled look on Sam's face as Ross went storming past her.

Leaving her secretary in midsentence, Sam rushed back into her office. "What happened?"

"I don't know," Sharon murmured distractedly. "It all happened so fast."

"What did he say?"

She brushed the bangs out of her eyes as if that would clear up the confusion in her mind. "He apologized for what he did to me, he said he could never forgive himself and...and before I could say a word he went storming out the door."

"Hell!" Sam exclaimed, following Ross's receding back with her eyes. "That proud, stubborn, idealistic...idiot!" She turned and glared at Sharon with the same loving outrage. "Well, don't just stand there!" Grabbing her by the shoulders, she propelled her over to the door. "Go get him!"

Ross finished towel-drying his hair and tossed the towel aside with a disgusted gesture. The cold shower had refreshed his body after the long, hot drive in traffic back to

St. Michaels but hadn't eased his mind. Seeing Sharon earlier had been like ripping the scab off a still fresh wound,
leaving him raw with pain.

He combed his damp hair with impatient fingers then
slipped into his terry cloth robe on his way out of the bathroom. Stopping only to get a chilled can of beer from the
refrigerator, he continued into the main room. A deep sigh
escaped him when he looked around: the cabin had never
seemed emptier.

He should have stayed in his apartment in Baltimore, he
told himself irritably; it was just as empty but at least it held
no memories to torment him. He knew there was no point
in his staying at the cabin during the week any longer, yet
every night since Sharon had left he'd made the long drive
in traffic from the city. Every night he'd waited for the
knock on the door that had never come. He'd stopped
expecting it.

Ross hadn't realized that he'd been wandering aimlessly
around the room until he found himself in front of his open
desk. The research notes he'd compiled on Bob Crane's
tragic death were still waiting to be sorted out, the article
was still waiting to be written. For the first time in his life,
he was unable to lose himself in his work.

Lifting the icy can to his lips, Ross took a long swig of
beer. The cold shower was supposed to have shaken him out
of his depression so he could do some work, he reminded
himself impatiently; his deadline was only a week away.
With a raw curse, he slammed the beer can down on the desk
and seated himself. Reaching into the top drawer, he pulled
out a sheet of white typing paper.

Suddenly, as Ross was rolling the sheet of paper into the
typewriter, Sharon's image flashed into his mind, her eyes
dark with the pain of betrayal, the page she'd just finished

reading trembling in her hand. The roller spun wildly as he ripped the page out of the typewriter. Crushing it in one hand, he threw it angrily. The crumpled ball of paper ricocheted off the window behind his desk.

For several long minutes, Ross stared blindly out the window as memories of Sharon, her face transfigured, her delicate body shaking uncontrollably in his arms as he made love to her, filled every corner of his mind. He was unaware of the fiery colors of the sunset fading into an indigo-blue dusk or of the dark shadows spilling into the study—until he saw the electric light go on across the way.

For an instant, he thought it was just his imagination. But it wasn't an illusion, the light *was* on in Sharon's bedroom. Sitting up, he peered intently through the window. Through the spaces between the pine trees, he could make out her white Jaguar convertible in the driveway.

She must have driven up while he was in the shower, he realized, or he would have heard her. One by one, all the lights in her house went on until it glowed like a Christmas tree. He couldn't understand why she'd turned on all the lights...unless she *wanted* him to know she was back. Before he could decide what to do, the lantern over the back door flashed on, and Sharon stepped outside.

For a moment, Ross thought his heart had stopped, then it began racing to make up for the skipped beats. Without thinking, he rushed over to the cabin door and pulled it open. He hadn't taken more than a few steps outside when he came to a stunned halt. A full moon hung low in the sky. Just beginning its slow ascent into the star-studded heavens, it suffused earth and water in an unreal glow. Ross watched Sharon moving toward him as in a dream—a dream he never wanted to wake from.

Satin rustled around her ankles like the leaves swaying in the breeze when she turned suddenly and glided down the grassy embankment.

Ross called out Sharon's name when he saw her step onto the pier. When she didn't answer, he went rushing down the grassy slope after her. She paused when she reached the open end of the pier. The ivory robe slid off her shoulders, down her back and legs to fall in a shimmering pool around her feet. Ross's breath caught when he saw that she was naked, slowing him down. Her pale, delicate body appeared as luminous and insubstantial as a moonbeam. When she kicked off her slippers and went up on her toes, he broke into a run, but she was too quick for him. By the time he got there, she was a flash of creamy flesh breaking the moonlit reflection on the water before becoming part of it.

"Sharon?" Ross cried as he pulled off his own robe and slippers. Quickly, he searched the waters to make sure she'd come out of the dive safely but the moon had been swallowed up by clouds, plunging everything into darkness. "Are you all right?"

Her answer was a laugh, sensuous and inviting, floating up to him on the warm, pine-scented breeze.

He breathed a sigh that mingled relief with exasperation. "Where are you?"

"Over here," she called up to him just as the moon evaded the clouds. "Come and get me."

Sharon's teasing smile faded. Something turned over inside her as she watched Ross setting himself to dive, moonlight pouring down the long, hard lines of his naked body. She was never more aware of his purely male grace and power than she was at that instant or of the effect it had on her. When he went into the dive his body seemed to hang in space for an endless moment, every taut sleek muscle gleaming, before it disappeared beneath the dark waters.

He came up mere inches away from her. She was waiting.

Grabbing her roughly around the waist, he pulled her up against his side. "Don't worry, I've got you."

Sharon was anything but worried. Ross was too concerned about her welfare to notice.

"Get on my back," he ordered, "so I can get you away from this current."

The current was as strong as Sharon remembered but she wasn't having any trouble fighting it because the water was warm now and she was a very good swimmer. But since Ross was determined to rescue her, she obeyed him without a word.

She felt powerful muscles tauten under her when she slipped onto his back, skin sliding wetly on skin. Wrapping her arms around his chest, she clung to him, eager for the feel of his lean, hard body. Her own body felt weightless in the water yet more firmly anchored to life than it had ever been.

"Let's not go all the way in," Sharon murmured when they were halfway there, her breath brushing the side of his face, her body bobbing softly on top of him. "Not yet. This is delightful."

Ross couldn't have agreed with her more even though he was so confused by everything that was happening that he could hardly think straight. "It's safe over here," he managed, halting. "And shallow enough so we can stand."

With his long legs, Ross had no trouble finding the bottom. Sharon was not so fortunate. She had to grab his shoulders to stay upright. She laughed, flicking the wet hair out of her face. "You keep forgetting that not everyone has long legs like you."

"I really should be mad as hell at you," Ross said, wrapping his arms around her waist to hold her securely against him. He'd meant to keep his tone and manner stern but it was impossible to resist that bubbly, childlike laugh of hers, the irrepressible glow that lit up her face, making it more radiant than the moonlight. "You know how strong the current is out there. Why did you do that?"

"Because I wanted to go back to the beginning," she explained with a purely female logic, love and humor blending in the dark depths of her eyes. "Maybe if we start over at the beginning, we can get it right this time." Her slender arms went up to wind around his neck. "It'll be a *new* beginning for us."

Ross staggered back a step, sending the water lapping around their waists. "A new beginning?" he murmured, almost afraid to believe what he was hearing.

"Yes, and a kind of...baptism." Pulling her legs up easily in the buoyant water, she wrapped them around his waist, freeing her arms. Scooping water with slivers of moonlight in it, she raised her hands over his head. Slowly, she let it drip through her fingers. "To wash the past away so we can start fresh." Scooping up another handful of water impulsively, she let it pour down over her own head. "I want to be reborn...in you."

"Yes!" Ross crushed her to him, water sliding between their bodies as he took her mouth in a fierce kiss.

Throwing her arms around him, Sharon returned his kiss with every part of her. A shiver went through her when she felt the deep possessive thrust of his tongue; like ripples on water it spread in ever-widening circles to her farthest nerve ending.

"I just want to know one thing," Ross drawled when he finally dragged his mouth away from hers. Love and laughter made his eyes gleam once more like burnished gold. "Are you planning on diving off the deep end of the pier every time there's a full moon?"

Sharon laughed breathlessly. "Only if you're there to catch me."

"I will be," he vowed, sealing his promise with a kiss that was all hunger and desperation as he started carrying her out of the water. "Don't ever leave me again," he murmured against her lips.

"Never!" Sharon promised.

His arms tightened around her and his mouth took hers again, hot and hard, branding her, making her his completely, irrevocably. For all time.

If you're ready for a more sensual, more provocative reading experience...

We'll send you
4 Silhouette Desire novels
FREE
and without obligation

Then, we'll send you six more Silhouette Desire® novels to preview every month for 15 days with absolutely no obligation!

When you decide to keep them, you pay just $1.95 each ($2.25 each in Canada) *with never any additional charges!*

And that's not all. You get FREE home delivery of all books as soon as they are published and a FREE subscription to the Silhouette Books Newsletter as long as you remain a member. Each issue is filled with news on upcoming titles, interviews with your favorite authors, even their favorite recipes.

Silhouette Desire novels are not for everyone. They are written especially for the woman who wants a more satisfying, more deeply involving reading experience. Silhouette Desire novels take you *beyond* the others.

If you're ready for that kind of experience, fill out and return the coupon today!

Silhouette ❤ Desire®

Silhouette Books, 120 Brighton Rd., P.O. Box 5084, Clifton, NJ 07015-5084

Clip and mail to: Silhouette Books,
120 Brighton Road, P.O. Box 5084, Clifton, NJ 07015-5084 *

YES. Please send me 4 FREE Silhouette Desire novels. Unless you hear from me after I receive them, send me 6 new Silhouette Desire novels to preview each month as soon as they are published. I understand you will bill me just $1.95 each, a total of $11.70 (in Canada, $2.25 each, a total of $13.50)—with no additional shipping, handling, or other charges of any kind. There is no minimum number of books that I must buy, and I can cancel at any time. The first 4 books are mine to keep.   **BD18R6**

Name   (please print)

Address   Apt. #

City   State/Prov.   Zip/Postal Code

* In Canada, mail to: Silhouette Canadian Book Club, 320 Steelcase Rd., E., Markham, Ontario, L3R 2M1, Canada
Terms and prices subject to change.
SILHOUETTE DESIRE is a service mark and registered trademark.   D-SUB-1

Silhouette Brings You:

Silhouette Christmas Stories

Four delightful, romantic stories celebrating the holiday season, written by four of your favorite Silhouette authors.

Nora Roberts—*Home for Christmas*
Debbie Macomber—*Let It Snow*
Tracy Sinclair—*Under the Mistletoe*
Maura Seger—*Starbright*

Each of these great authors has combined the wonder of falling in love with the magic of Christmas to bring you four unforgettable stories to touch your heart.

Indulge yourself during the holiday season ... or give this book to a special friend for a heartwarming Christmas gift.

Available November 1986

XMAS-1

Silhouette Desire

**Available
October 1986**

California Copper

The second in an exciting new
Desire Trilogy by Joan Hohl.

If you fell in love with Thackery—the
laconic charmer of *Texas Gold*—you're
sure to feel the same about his twin
brother, Zackery.

In *California Copper*, Zackery meets the
beautiful Aubrey Mason on the windswept
Pacific coast. Tormented by memories,
Aubrey has only to trust . . . to embrace
Zack's flame . . . and he can ignite the fire in
her heart.

The trilogy continues when you
meet Kit Aimsley, the twins' half
sister, in *Nevada Silver*. Look for
Nevada Silver—coming soon from
Silhouette Books.

DT-B-1

FOUR UNIQUE SERIES
FOR EVERY WOMAN YOU ARE...

Silhouette Romance

Heartwarming romances that will make you laugh and cry as they bring you all the wonder and magic of falling in love.

6 titles per month

Silhouette Special Edition

Expanded romances written with emotion and heightened romantic tension to ensure powerful stories. A rare blend of passion and dramatic realism.

6 titles per month

Silhouette Desire

Believable, sensuous, compelling—and above all, romantic—these stories deliver the promise of love, the guarantee of satisfaction.

6 titles per month

Silhouette Intimate Moments

Love stories that entice; longer, more sensuous romances filled with adventure, suspense, glamour and melodrama.

4 titles per month

Silhouette Romances
not available in retail outlets in Canada

SIL-GEN-1A